Dogsbody

&

other strange tales

Moya Green

Published in 2013 by FeedARead.com Publishing —
Arts Council funded

A CIP catalogue record for this title is available from
the British Library.

Contents:

Dogsbody *published in Voices from the Web 1, Boho Press, 2003*

A Better Place? *1ˢᵗ place, Christchurch Writers' Circle Short Story Competition, 2002*

The Wishfish *3ʳᵈ place, March & Doddington Writers' Circle Competition 2002. Published in The Quill 2002*

All the Little Teddy Bears. *1ˢᵗ place, Christchurch WC Competition 2001. Published inVoices from the Web 1, Boho Press. 2003*

Flabberghast *2ⁿᵈ place, Redcar Writers open competition 2001*

I lost my heart in Wolverhampton. *Shortlisted, Jo Cowell Award 2002*

Dogsbody

It was on the night of the great thunderstorm that George finally decided to become a dog.

He was used to sharing the marital bed with Topsy the poodle and Flopsy the Clumber spaniel; but when, frightened by the thunder, Mopsy the old English sheepdog joined them it all became too much of a crowd and George was summarily ejected onto the bedroom floor.

'That's it,' George thought as he curled up in Mopsy's basket. 'I've had enough. I'll make an appointment first thing in the morning.'

The doctor, when George eventually got to see him, was dubious. 'It's a major procedure, a species-change operation. Have you discussed this with your wife?'

'Of course,' lied George, suppressing a smile. One did not discuss things like that with Beryl. Or anything else for that matter. No, it would be a nice surprise for her. He hoped she would like him better as a dog. Certainly she did not have much use for him as a man.

'I can get you an appointment with the specialist,' said the doctor, 'but it might take a while. And you do realize they are not funding this sort of thing on the NHS any more? You would have to have it done privately.'

It was rather more than George could afford, but he thought it well worth the money. A few weeks later

Beryl's dog-walking friends in the park were able to admire the new addition to the family.

'Yes, that's George,' replied Beryl, gazing fondly. 'I've never really taken to small dogs, but I have to admit, he's a perky little fellow.'

George settled easily into his new life. He was slightly disappointed by his breed - he had fancied something like a Doberman or German Shepherd, but the specialist had explained that his new incarnation had to reflect his former personality and physique, and being a Jack Russell was not too bad. His small size meant that the double bed was now big enough for all of them, and George felt welcome there for the first time in years. The food was good - gourmet dog-food was a distinct improvement on Beryl's cooking. She still expected instant obedience, so there was nothing new there, but at least now he got a pat on the head and a murmured 'Good boy!'.

Of course, life wasn't all walkies and doggichox. The other dogs did not really take to him. They had always despised him, and now they were all so much bigger than he was; but he was used to female domination. They were not the real problem. No, what lay at the root of his trouble was sex.

He had been warned that there might be some increase in libido, but had not paid much attention. He had never been terribly interested in his former life, but now he was a Jack Russell he seemed to think of little else. Topsy, Flopsy and Mopsy were no use to him at all in that department. They had all had the operation. As for getting out to search for more accommodating bitches, Beryl was even stricter about that sort of thing than when he had been a man. She no longer let him off the lead in the park, after that unfortunate incident with the Great Dane.

This continual sexual frustration led to a serious deterioration in his temper. He became irritable and snappy, aggressive towards strangers, especially visitors to the house. No postman dared approach the door. There were outbreaks of mindless vandalism directed against Beryl's clothes and soft furnishings. However his anger was never aimed at Beryl herself. Her, he adored. Totally.

He had never appreciated the true meaning of the phrase 'dog-like devotion' until he became a dog. He had always admired a masterful woman, that was what had drawn him to Beryl in the first place, but now he worshipped her. Praise from her set his tail wagging in ecstasies of delight, while a harsh word reduced him to abject misery. To share her with others became a torment to him. He was her knight, her protector, keeping the world at bay. He could not see, in his blind infatuation, that it was the very excess of his devotion that was alienating her. After all, he was only a dog.

So at last the day came when Beryl went to the park accompanied as usual by Flopsy, Mopsy and Topsy - but no George.

'It all got too much for me,' she replied to the enquiries of her friends. 'You know how fond I was of the little chap. But he became impossibly jealous, always picking fights. It was starting to affect the others. I couldn't have that. We used to be such a happy little family. And he was so destructive. I tried taking him to a canine psychiatrist, but there was nothing to be done. He was too old to change, he could only get worse.

'Found him a new home? Oh no, that would have been cruel. He was strictly a one-woman dog. He would have pined away. No, it was a hard decision, but in the end I really had no choice. It was the kindest thing to do, for George as well as me.'

Beryl wiped away a tear. 'And I still have him, in a way. I couldn't bear to part with him completely, so afterwards I took him to that place off the High Street, and they did a marvellous job. He does look sweet on the back shelf of the car.

'Yes, that's right. I've had him stuffed.'

A better place?

The day Neville finally dropped off his perch he was so plastered it took him some time to notice. When he eventually became aware of his surroundings he found himself lying at the foot of a deep shaft. Far above was a faint circle of light.

'Some stupid bugger's left a manhole cover off,' he thought.

After a while it dawned on him that he ought to do something about it. He clambered to his feet, and realised that the shaft was not vertical as he had first thought, but inclined at an angle of about forty-five degrees. He should be able to climb out.

It was a painful crawl and for a long time the light seemed to come no nearer, but at last he reached the top and was able to squeeze out into the open. He gasped. He was standing before an immense wall, pierced by hundreds of turnstile gates. A long queue stretched from each gate. It reminded him of a football stadium - but far vaster than anything he could ever have imagined.

'Must be a big game,' he thought as he joined the nearest queue.

'Name? Date of birth?' snapped the ticket clerk. 'Date of death?'

Neville gaped. Death? 'What is this place?' he stuttered.

'The Pearly Gates of course.'

'What, all of the them?'

'Certainly. Can't process the numbers we get through nowadays with just one set.' The clerk twitched his wings impatiently. 'Hurry along now, I haven't got all eternity. Through the barrier and turn left.'

Neville took the ticket thrust at him and pushed through the turnstile.

'Numbers 28,000,035 to 28,000,050 this way' shouted a small angel.

Neville glanced down at his ticket. 28,000,047. He tagged along behind a motley group of people. They were all wearing whatever they had died in, so most were in nightwear of various descriptions. Many wore ordinary clothes, some of which were torn and had bits missing. There was a man in a wet-suit, and a woman in riding clothes, and one fat bloke in some very strange leather items, all trussed up in chains. Neville glance down at himself, then sighed with relief. His torn jeans and dirty t-shirt were no worse than usual.

'You wouldn't happen to have a fag on you?

Neville jumped. The small angel had dropped back and was walking beside him. He was not quite Neville's idea of an angel. His wing feathers appeared to be moulting, and from the look of his robes, his mother didn't use Persil.

'Yeah, sure.' He fished out his packet and offered it. They both lit up.

'Ah, that's better,' said the angel. 'I could look after these for you,' he added. 'You won't be allowed to take them inside. Heaven's a smoke-free zone, now.

'I suppose so,' said Neville. 'By the way, something's been puzzling me. How come I've ended up here? I thought I'd have qualified for the other place.'

'Oh, it's all one since the Rationalisation,' said the angel. 'The Powers That Be decided it was too expensive to run separate establishments, so they closed

Hell down and now everyone's sent here. Only the sinners don't enjoy it.'

Neville's attention had been distracted by a young lady who had just joined their party - blonde, shapely and stark naked. He frowned, worried. A sight like that - something should be happening to him, but nothing stirred.

'Shit,' he muttered. 'I really am dead!'

''Fraid so,' said the angel.

'So what happens now?'

'First you get Washed in the Blood of the Lamb.'

'Sounds disgusting.'

'You come out nice and clean. Then you get your robes and join the Blessed. Are you musical?'

'I used to play the tenor sax.'

'Sorry, not allowed. Only harps and trumpets here. Well,' he turned to go, 'better get back and round up another batch. No rest for the wicked! See you around, maybe.'

They had reached a large building strongly resembling a municipal swimming bath. Neville watch the angel fly away, feeling suddenly lost and lonely, before following the others inside.

The Blood of the Lamb was not as bad as he expected, more like a shower of red scented water, and it certainly cleaned him up. He was rather annoyed to see all his tattoos had disappeared. He'd been proud of them, especially the naked lady on his chest. When he flexed his muscles he could get her to - well, couldn't be helped. He pulled on the regulation white nightshirt and went outside.

Two elderly ladies were waiting for him, each with identical tightly-permed grey hair and beaming smiles.

'Mam!' he cried. 'And Auntie Ginny. How - how lovely.'

He found himself pressed to his mother's meagre bosom. 'Neville, love! We came as soon as we heard you'd Passed Over. I never though I'd ever see you here.' She wiped a surreptitious tear from her eye.

'Didn't think you'd make it, see,' said Auntie Ginny. 'But then,' she went on with a disapproving sniff, 'they let all sorts in nowadays.'

'Come along, you must be hungry.' fussed his mother. 'I can tell you're not eating properly. And your hair! When did you last have it cut?'

They led him to a table, covered in plates of sliced bread and flagons of water.

'Is this all?' asked Neville.

'Bread of Heaven and Living Water,' said his mother. 'What more could you want?'

'Bit of butter would be nice.' He picked up a slice and nibbled it. It tasted like - well - bread. He poured a glass of the Living Water, drank it off, then gasped in astonishment and horror. He was instantly, totally, sober. The comforting fog which, for most of his adult life, had shielded him from reality had vanished, and he had the uncomfortable feeling that it would not be back.

He looked round. They were in a green meadow, under a cloudless blue sky. Around him the newly arrived were being greeted by their long-lost friends and relations. Others of the Blessed wandered aimlessly about. There were animals too - he could see the lion lying down with the lamb, and the horses of the Apocalypse grazed peacefully a little way away. He noticed many of the Blessed wore fixed expressions of total bliss.

'What are they on?' he muttered.

'They have gone before the Throne, and been touched by the Hand of the Lord,' said his mother.

'Thought they looked a bit touched,' agreed Neville.

'You'll be going, once you're ready,' said Auntie Ginny. 'You're Mam and I have been sent to be your guides, to prepare you.'

'But don't worry,' went on his mother, 'there's plenty to do while you're waiting. There's Singing the Praises of the Lord, loads of prayer meetings, and for a treat we have Socials, and sometimes one of the Archangels comes and gives a lecture. With slides.'

'Doesn't sound much fun.'

'Fun?' His mother was scandalised. 'This is the place of Eternal Bliss. You're not supposed to have fun!'

'I can see you still have plenty of Sinful Habits that need eradicating,' said Auntie Ginny. 'But don't worry. Just do whatever your Mam says and you'll be all right. Now finish up your bread and water or we'll be late for Community Hymn Singing.'

Several eternities later Neville happened to bump into the dingy angel again. 'You wouldn't still have those ciggies I gave you?' he asked.

'Not the same ones, but I manages to cadge another packet,' said the angel. 'come round the back of the Rock of Ages and we'll have a quiet smoke.'

'How are you doing?' asked the angel as they lit up.

'Terrible!' groaned Neville. 'It's the hymns that get me. They just don't let up. I think if I have to sing 'Here no night brings rest from labour' one more time I'll get the screaming habdabs. And when we're not singing they make us go to a sort of Sunday School to learn about heaven. D'you know, we have to know the names of all the angels! What's yours, by the way?'

'Shax - I mean, Ezriel,' said the angel. Neville looked at him, and he hastily twitched his robe to cover - could it possibly be - a cloven hoof?

'You're not - you're never - ?' gasped Neville.

The angel blushed. 'OK, I admit it, I used to work Down Below. Most of us were made redundant or took early retirement when Hell closed down, but a few were relocated. It's not what I was used to, but at least it's a job.'

'But how can you stand it here? It's so boring! It's not fair, no matter what I did on earth, it wasn't bad enough to deserve this.'

'You'll get used to it.'

'I don't want to get used to it. I want out.' A celestial trumpet sounded and Neville groaned again.

'Supper-time. More Bread of Heaven. I could kill for a bag of chips!'

Shax/Ezriel looked round furtively, then leaned forward. 'I shouldn't really be telling you this,' he whispered, 'but you seem a decent sort. There is a way Downstairs. They didn't seal of Hell completely, you see. Wouldn't have been safe, with all those lakes of burning sulphur. There's a skeleton staff, for basic maintenance. Some of us pop down on our days off. The place isn't what it was, of course, but there's a pub, and a chip shop, and a couple of bookies.'

'Sounds great,' breathed Neville. 'How do I get there?'

'You'll have to be brave. The way is guarded.'

'Dragons?'

'In a manner of speaking.'

'I don't care,' declared Neville. 'I'm desperate.'

'OK. Go down the Valley of the Shadow . . . '

The towering cliffs of the Valley of the Shadow of Death closed in. He must be near the place. A cave, Shax/Ezriel had said, leading to a shaft going down. Yes, there ...

'And where do you think you are going?'

Neville stopped, aghast. His mother had materialised between him and the cave mouth.

'Out,' he said.

'Out where?'

'Just out,' he repeated sulkily.

'Have you finished your homework?'

'Yes.'

'Really? Recite the names of the angels of the order of Thrones.'

'Er - ' Neville's mind blanked.

'I thought not! Get back to your room, and don't come downstairs again till you're word perfect.'

Neville made a dash for the cave, but a hand snaked out and grabbed him by the collar. She seemed to have grown to three times her former size. 'Oh no you don't! Off to play mummies and daddies, were you, with that Sadie down the road? Nasty, dirty little boy. I'm going to paddle your behind!'

He ducked under her arm, and with a supreme effort wrenched himself free and gained the cave mouth.

'Neville, love, you wouldn't leave your poor old Mam?' The quavering voice followed him. In spite of himself he looked back.

She had shrunk again, into a frail old lady, holding out her arms beseechingly. 'You wouldn't break your mother's heart and drive her to an early grave?'

'I think I did that already,' said Neville. He turned away, took a step - and found himself falling into darkness.

The fall was long enough for him to think 'I'm going to die!' and then 'I am dead, stupid'. Unfortunately he discovered when he reached the bottom that he could still be hurt, and it was some time before he felt like taking stock of his surroundings. When he did he found himself lying on a mound of cinders. Everywhere was shrouded in a darkness, a great relief after the perpetual day of Heaven. The only light came from a burning lake in the distance, which the low clouds reflected with a sullen glow, and the neon signs on a the cluster of building at the foot of the mound. A path led towards them. Neville picked himself up and limped painfully down. After a few yards he nearly fell over a figure sprawled on the path.

It wore a leather miniskirt and fishnet stockings. A Fallen Woman, obviously. He picked her up.

Not long after he was sitting comfortably in the Lounge of the 'Furnace Arms' with a pint of 'Old Nick' in front of him and the Fallen Woman opposite. Brenda, she said her name was. Seemed a nice girl. She reminded him of his lost tattoo. Firelight gleamed on the highly polished instruments of torture decorating the walls, and on the horns of the demon barmaid. A jukebox blared heavy metal in one corner, while in another a television screen showed the racing. Neville could not quite make out what animals they were riding - not horses, too many legs. Not too worry. Brenda was smiling at him across the table, showing a generous amount of cleavage, and judging from the noise a fight had just started in the Public Bar. Neville raised his glass, and sighed with contentment.

'Heaven,' he said

Frog Off

She opened her handbag. The frog was still there.

'Can I come out now?'

'You might as well,' said Mabel. They were in the garret room which she shared with the other scullery maids.

The frog hopped onto her bedside table. He was quite handsome, as frogs go: emerald green with a yellow stripe down each side. He expanded his throat, in that unnerving way frogs do, and croaked.

'Don't do that!' hissed Mabel. 'You'll wake everyone. Oh dear, whatever am I going to do with you? I thought you were a prince. I'd never have let you kiss me if you hadn't been a prince.'

'I am a prince,' said the frog. 'At least, I was.'

'Then it's princesses you should be kissing, not scullery maids,' said Mabel.

The frog sighed. 'It's not working out, between me and the princess. She says she needs someone with a fiery, passionate nature – I'm too cold-blooded'. He sniffed. 'She said I was wet.'

'That's a shame.'

'So I thought, if kissing a princess turned me into a prince, perhaps kissing someone who wasn't a princess might turn me back into a frog.'

''Was that the only reason you kissed me?' Mabel felt a bit miffed.

'Oh – er – I thought you were very pretty. Obviously. Anyway, it worked.'

'So what now? I can't keep you here. Pets aren't allowed.'

'I need to return to my pond, but I'm not sure how to get there. Can you help me? Please, please, pretty scullery maid,' pleaded the frog. 'I don't even know how to get out of the palace without being squashed.'

'Don't cry,' said Mabel. 'It'll make you even damper. I'll help, but you'll have to wait till tomorrow, I'm not traipsing around in the dark.'

She put him in her soap-dish, covered him with a damp flannel, and went to bed.

Next morning Mabel got up early, before the other girls were awake, and looked in the soap dish. The frog was gone.

That's a relief, she thought. He must have decided to find his own way home. But as she was finishing getting dressed there came a terrible shriek from the loo. She rushed in to find one of the other girls gibbering with fright and pointing a shaking finger at the frog, which sat on the toilet seat rim looking embarrassed. Without hesitation, Mabel scooped him up.

'I'll see to this,' she said.

She carried him outside and down the stairs. 'Whatever were you trying to do?'

'I thought it might be a way out,' said the frog, 'but I got stuck in the U-bend. Then just as I had nearly climbed out, this person came and did something *unspeakable* . . .' he shuddered.

Mabel made a mental note to wash her hands as soon as possible. She put him in her pocket then went to the kitchen and collected a bucket from the scullery.

'I'll fetch the water to scrub the floor,' she told the under-kitchenmaid. Once outside, she dumped the bucket by the well.

'Where do you want to go?' she asked.

'The lily pond in the sunken garden, please,' replied the frog.

Mabel crept through the palace gardens, keeping an eye out for the gardeners, as kitchen staff were not supposed to be outside. She had almost reached the lily pond when –

'Oi! Who are you?'

She looked up to find a girl glaring at her. A girl in a very posh dress with a diamond encrusted crown on her head. It was the princess.

'Please, miss, I mean your Highness, I'm a scullery-maid . . . '

'This is outrageous,' cried the princess. 'A nasty, dirty scullery-maid in my private garden. I never heard the like!'

'I'm not dirty,' said Mabel indignantly.

'No, she's not,' said the frog, popping his head

out of her pocket. 'And she's not doing any harm. I asked her to take me home.'

'I know you,' said the princess. 'You're my – why've you turned back into a frog?'

'I'd had enough of being a prince. It happened when I kissed her.'

'You kissed *her*,' squealed the princess, going red in the face. 'You're my fiancé, you're supposed to kiss me!'

'Well I'd rather kiss her,' said the frog. 'She's not so bad-tempered. And she's prettier.'

'How dare you, that's treason. High Treason! I'll have her thrown in a dungeon, I'll have her beheaded. I'll have you squashed. Guards, guards!' The princess stormed off in a terrible temper.

'Oh dear, I have got you into trouble, haven't I?' said the frog. 'Can she really do all that?'

'Dunno. I expect she can get me sacked, anyway.' Mabel sighed. 'Just for trying to do someone a good turn. There's no justice in the world.'

'I'm awfully sorry. I wish there was something I could do.'

'It's not your fault. I don't blame you for not wanting to marry her. You'd better get back in your pond before she comes back and squashes you.'

He hopped onto the rim of the pond. 'Thank you for everything. Can I kiss you goodbye?'

'Why not?' She bent down, felt his cold lips touch her, and then -

Something very strange began to happen to her. Her clothes became much too large, and fell off, but she didn't mind. Her body shrank, her legs became longer and her skin turned a fetching shade of green.

'Goodness me,' she croaked. She joined the frog on the pond rim. Yes, she thought, he is extremely handsome.

'Wow!' he said. 'You're even prettier as a frog.'

He took her hand and together they jumped into the lily pond, where they lived happily ever after. Frogs, Mabel found, have a much easier life than scullery-maids.

The Spirits of Christmas

'Twas the night before Christmas, and all through the house not a creature – hang on. What was that?

A low moaning eddied through the darkness of Grimleigh Hall, rising to a bubbling shriek before subsiding to a whimper. It was enough to turn a strong man into a gibbering wreck from sheer terror, except that all the strong men in the vicinity were snoring like pigs.

'I don't know why I bother,' said the White Lady in disgust, as she drifted through the wall into the dining room.

The Headless Horseman sneezed, and parked his head on the sideboard while he rummaged for a hanky.

'I know,' he said. 'No-one appreciates us traditional ghosts these days. It's all zombies and sexy vampires nowadays.'

A faint rattling could now be heard, coming nearer, until someone else came through the door without bothering to open it.

'Hi, Clanker,' said Headless. 'Glad you could make it. Where's Polly?'

The recently arrived spectre heaved his ball and chain onto the sofa and collapsed beside it with a sigh. 'I swear that thing gets heavier every year. Polly will be along in a minute. She's just giving the skeleton in the cupboard a bit of a shake up.'

The White Lady sniffed. 'I don't know why we keep inviting that poltergeist female. So brash and noisy. She does lower the tone.'

'Don't be unfriendly,' said Clanker. 'There's no harm in her – and it is Christmas.'

Polly blew in to the accompaniment of plates leaping off the sideboard and the clock striking thirteen and the annual Christmas Eve party commenced.

The table was loaded with the Ghost of Christmas Dinners Past, while wine flowed copiously from dead bottles. After dinner they went through the wall into the Blue Drawing Room. Polly switched the telly on and they settled down to watch reruns of 'Terry and June'.

'I love a scary programme,' said the White Lady.

Time went by in a somnolent haze until –

'Listen!' hissed the Headless Horseman. ''What's that noise?'

'It's coming from the Great Hall,' cried the White Lady.

It was but the work of a moment to relocate themselves. A strange grunting sound was coming from the enormous hearth, accompanied by showers of soot.

''D'you think it's Santa Claus?' whispered Polly.

'Don't be daft,' said Clanker. 'Santa Claus isn't real.'

'Well, *he* looks real enough,' snapped the Lady.

A pair of boots had appeared in the fireplace, followed by a portly figure in red, clutching a large sack.

'It can't be!' gasped Polly.

'No it can't,' said the Headless Horseman. 'That beard's false for a start.'

The strange man looked around, listening, then crept towards the end of the hall where the immense Christmas tree stood, its base piled high with presents. As the ghosts watched in amazement, he began shoving parcels into his sack.

'He's not Father Christmas,' said Clanker. 'He's a burglar!'

'We must scare him away.' The White Lady let out a soul-destroying shriek as she swept towards – and straight through – the intruder.

The Horseman waved his head, which was gurning furiously, while Clanker tried to bash him with his ball and a chain, but it was all to no avail. The false Santa never turned a whisker. He nicked the last parcel and added the candlesticks from the mantelpiece.

'Huh!' snorted Polly. 'Right wastes of ectoplasm you lot are. Leave this to the expert.'

She began to revolve, faster and faster until she became a vortex of pure energy. Strange things began to happen. Santa squawked in fright as a halberd detached itself from the wall and whizzed by his head to bury itself in the fire surround. A tiger skin rug at the end of the hall got to its feet and started to stalk him, growling. An unseen hand tugged his beard away from his face and let it snap back. Then all the buttons flew from his braces to ping against the far wall. It was too much. He dropped the sack and, clutching his trousers, fled to the front door. The bolts obligingly drew back as he approached and he staggered out into the drive where waited, not a sleigh and reindeer, but a dirty white van.

'I think that's the last we'll see of him,' said Clanker.

'Well done, Polly,' said Headless.

'Good show,' agreed the Lady.

Polly finished revolving. 'Don't mention it, haven't had so much fun since the 4th Earl caught his britches in the Iron Maiden. Could do with a lie down, though. Takes it out of me, this sort of thing.'

'I think I can hear the family stirring,' said Headless. 'I suppose even our lot couldn't sleep through this kerfuffle.'

The Lady sighed. 'Yes, there'll be no more peace tonight. Might as well return to our graves. Still, it was a lovely party.'

'Yes, quite exciting,' said Clanker. 'Ah, well, back to the dungeon. Merry Christmas, all.'

'Merry Christmas,' murmured the others.

And they all gently dematerialised, as the first hint of dawn crept over the horizon.

Flabberghast

The funny thing was, I'd never thought of myself as having a weight problem. Big, yes, all my family are, but I was tall enough to carry it. Martin, that's my boyfriend, he didn't mind.

'I like something I can get hold of,' he'd say.

He wanted me to move in with him - he has one of those new town houses just off the square, in fact that's how we met, when I took him to view it - but I wasn't quite ready for that and besides, I'd only just bought my new flat.

I'd had my eye on that flat for ages. The girl who'd lived there had died, and it was empty for a long while after, some sort of legal hassle I think, but as soon as it came on the market I snapped it up. One advantage of working in an estate agent's!

It was a lovely flat, just round the corner from work, ever so convenient. Big living-room. Fitted kitchen, brand-new bathroom, bedroom with en suite shower . . . The thing I liked most about the bedroom was the long mirror fixed to one wall. I'd never had a full-length mirror before, and you can never get a proper idea of what you look like when you only see yourself in bits.

I had Martin round for a meal soon after I moved in. I did chicken with mushrooms in a cream sauce. I got the recipe from a magazine, but I must have got the quantities wrong somehow. Martin ate his plateful all right (I like a man who enjoys his food), but

I could hardly get through half of mine. I put what was left in the fridge for next day, but then I didn't fancy it after all so it went in the bin. Shame, really.

I 'd been in the flat a couple of months when I first noticed that my clothes were getting a bit loose on me. When I bought new I had to get the next size down. All the girls at work complimented me and asked if I had been dieting, but I hadn't. I just didn't seem to want to eat as much as I used to. I'd never been one for breakfast, a couple of slices of hot buttered toast would do me, and if I felt peckish during the morning I'd pop out for a cream bun, but I went right off cakes and puddings and all that sort of thing. Also that was the time when we were so busy at work, with Mr Elbone being off with his leg; some days I'd work right through lunch and then when I got home and cooked my tea I'd feel too tired to eat it.

I really noticed how much less I was eating when I went home for the weekend. We've always had good appetites in my family, and my mum's roast beef and Yorkshire pud is something to dream about, but I got a shock when I saw how she had piled my plate up. I did my best to eat it, not to hurt her feelings, so that I felt bloated and uncomfortable, and I still got 'Joanne, are you sure you're not sickening for something?' all afternoon. I was glad to get back.

I mean, it's not healthy, stuffing yourself all the time. I felt much better now I had cut down. Mind you, I made an exception on my birthday. Martin took me out for a meal to a really nice restaurant. Italian, it was. I had the lot. Seafood starter, pasta, beef with mushrooms in wine sauce and finished off with one of those desserts with brandy and cream. I did enjoy myself.

Afterwards Martin wanted me to stay over at his place, but I had work next day so I made him take me back to the flat. It was just as well I did. I started to feel queasy as soon as I got inside, and I only just made it to the bathroom before everything came back up. It must have been the seafood, I thought.

I still felt groggy next morning, so I took the day off. I stayed in bed till lunchtime, then got up and had a shower, and it was while I was drying myself that I happened to look in the long mirror. I hadn't seen myself properly for ages. I was always in too much of a rush, and I suppose I'd got a bit complacent with everyone saying I was so much slimmer. I had a dreadful shock. All that fat! Rolls of it round my middle, boobs like melons, great white wobbly thighs, and as for my behind - I decided there and then to stop messing about and go on a real diet. I couldn't bear to look like that. It was disgusting.

Well, once I put my mind to something, I don't do it by halves. I was pleased with myself, the way I stuck to that diet. I didn't care what anyone said. I got a few snide remarks from the girls at work, but I took no notice. They were only jealous. Though I have to admit it annoyed me when Martin began to have a go at me as well. He would keep fussing, and I hate that.

In the end we had an awful row. He'd taken me out for dinner again (his birthday this time) to a very up-market Chinese place, and ordered the set meal for two, the most expensive one. Only the sight of so much food took all my appetite away. I could hardly force any of it down. Of course Martin noticed, and I could see he was upset. We left early and went back to his place, and as soon as we were there, he started.

'Joanne. I'm worried about you. I think you should see a doctor.'

'There's nothing wrong with me,' I said 'Just because I wasn't feeling hungry . . . '

'But you're never hungry! You never eat anything.'

Well, that was nonsense. I ate far too much, that was the trouble.

'This dieting has gone too far, it's got to stop,' he went on. 'We used to laugh at all those skinny models in magazines, but now you seem to be turning into one.'

That made me really angry. 'I suppose you liked me better before!'

'Yes, I did,' he said.

So I told him if he did not like the way I was now he'd better find someone else. Then I stormed out and took a taxi back to the flat. Just as well I had not given up my independence, I thought. The cheek! No man was going to tell me how to run my life. And how could he possibly say I was too thin? I only had to look in the mirror to see how fat I was.

He rang a few times, but I kept the answering machine on and he gave up eventually. I missed him, but not as much as I thought I would, because it was about then I found the notebook. I came across it in the airing cupboard, when I was poking around behind the cistern after some knickers which had dropped down. It was a kind of diary. I realised it must have belonged to the girl who'd had the flat before me. She was a dieter too, only better at it. Every day there was a list of meals with what she had eaten for each one, and a note of how much weight she had lost.

It was extraordinary, how anyone could exist on so little food. Well! I thought to myself. If she could do it, so can I. I began to use the notebook as my guide. I know it sounds quite mad now, but at the time it seemed a perfectly reasonable thing to do. It became a kind of competition between us, a game. If she had two dry crisp bread for breakfast, I'd have one. If her lunch was an apple, mine would be half. I could tell she approved. Towards the end I could almost feel her as an actual presence, warning me away from the fridge if I weakened, encouraging me when I felt down. I even made up a name for her. Flabberghast, I called her.

Then one day I was sitting in the loo at work. I'd felt a bit faint and gone to put my head between my knees. Two of the other girls came in. The didn't know I was there, of course.

'Well, we need to do something about Joanne. She looks ghastly, really ill.'

'I know, but what can you do? She simply won't admit there's a problem. We've all tried talking to her but we just can't get through.'

'I think Mr Elbone might have a word with her. I mean, it's getting to be bad for business. Only the other day a bloke started to come in, took one look and walked right out again.'

'Who'd blame him? I wouldn't want to be greeted by the Walking Skeleton.'

They both laughed and went out while I sat there shaking. How could they be so horrible? I thought they were my friends. As soon as I felt capable of moving I told Mr Elbone I wasn't well and went home.

Back at the flat I went straight to the mirror. The Walking Skeleton! It couldn't be true!

It was not true. My body was as I knew it would be - fat legs, fat tummy, fat face -

Only the face which stared out of the mirror was not mine.

I've no idea what happened next. Martin says I rang him at work, totally hysterical, and he rushed round to find me collapsed on the floor. All I remember is waking up in hospital.

They let me go after a few days. There was talk of a special clinic, but I didn't fancy that, and Martin said he would look after me. He was marvellous. He took me back to his place and nursed me and fed me, and somehow I never got round to moving out.

My appetite came back with a rush, so I've put half the weight back on. I had one problem left, though. The flat. I didn't need it now (and there's no way I would have lived there again anyway), but if I sold it I might not get my money back. Besides, I knew now what a lucky escape I'd had. It didn't seem fair to pass the problem on to some poor unsuspecting buyer.

Then one day when I was trying on a new dress, and thinking how nice it was to be a size fourteen instead of eighteen, I had my brilliant idea.

Since then that flat has become a little goldmine. I only let it for short-term tenancies, three to six months is ideal, and I vet all the tenants personally to make sure they are suitable. They have to be at least two stone overweight. I've never advertised, it's all done by personal recommendation, but you'd be surprised how word gets around. I even have a waiting list. I had a woman phone only this morning, sounding very keen. She'd got my number off a friend, one of my former tenants.

'I couldn't get over how well Betty was looking,' she kept saying. 'So much slimmer, I hardly recognised her. I was flabbergasted!'

Not yet, I thought, but don't worry. You will be.

I lost my heart in Wolverhampton

Valentine's Day, it was. I'd given him a lovely card, all hearts and flowers, and he'd bought me a rude one. I'd cooked him a special dinner, steak and chips and mushy peas, and got a bottle of wine to go with it. I even lit a couple of candles and put a red rose in a little vase on the table. Afterwards we sat on the settee with just the candles and the light from the telly. It was really nice and romantic.

Then he turns to me and says, 'Wanna shag?'

Bloody Vince! He always has to spoil things. And Coronation Street was starting. I mean, I wasn't being unreasonable. It was only half an hour to wait. There was no call to say all those nasty things. Like, I was a frigid cow who never wanted it anymore and lucky to get it the way I'd let myself go. And what my mother had to do with it all I'll never know. Frigid! Bloody cheek! Considering all that's on offer is staring at the ceiling for half an hour while he bangs away.

So he storms out in a huff, saying he's going down the pub, and I'm left there with my evening ruined. Sod it, I thought, I'm going out.

I put my coat on and walked down to the main road. It was a miserable night, wet and blowy, and there was hardly anyone about. A bus for the town centre stopped at the lights and I hopped on it. Only when I got there I didn't know what to do with myself. Everywhere was shut up. So there I am wandering around getting colder and colder and wondering what the hell I'm doing when I see this pub. I wouldn't normally go in on my own, in fact I've never been into one on my own, but I had to get out of that rain. And I was damned if I'd crawl back home with my tail between my legs.

The place was packed out, but I found a vacant stool at the end of the bar and ordered myself a Taboo and lemonade. Everyone else seemed to be in couples. The bar was all covered with cut-out paper hearts and there were heart-shaped balloons everywhere. I felt really conspicuous, like everyone was looking at me. I had to tell myself not to be silly, no-one was interested in me. Then I realised that somebody was. He was standing alone at the other end of the bar. As soon as he saw me looking he smiled and began to walk towards me. I must've sat there with my mouth hanging open. He was gorgeous - tall and slim, dark hair with a touch of silver at the temples, very distinguished. Expensive suit, lots of gold jewellery. It's no use, I can't describe him properly. Just think of any film star you really fancy, or the cover off a Mills and Boon and you'll get the idea. I mean, he wasn't real.

'Can I get you another drink?'

I looked down. My glass was empty, I'd drunk it without even noticing. I must have made some sort of noise, 'cos he snapped his fingers and two drinks appeared like magic.

'And how come someone as lovely as you is all alone on St Valentine's night?' he says.

Next thing I know, I'm telling him all about myself and Vince and what a pig he is, and he's nodding and smiling and gazing at me with those big brown eyes so I feel I'm drowning in them, and drinks keep appearing in front of me till all the colours in the room start to swirl around me. It must be late.

'I got to go,' I say.

'Nonsense,' he says, 'the night is young. Some friends of mine are having a party, why don't you come?'

So we go outside to his car. You never saw anything like it; driver in front, tinted windows, so long it must have to bend when it goes round corners. In the back there's a telly and a cocktail cabinet and enough room for a double bed if you'd wanted.

We sink down on soft leather seats and I rest my head on his shoulder, then he turns to me and our lips meet . . .

All too soon the car stops outside this big detached house. We get out and for a moment, only a moment, I feel there's something wrong somewhere. The house is all dark, uncurtained windows staring blankly. It looks dead. It certainly doesn't look as if there's a party going on.

I've half a mind to ask him to take me home, but the car's gone, slid away round the back somewhere. Then the door opens at his knock and there is a party after all, we're swept into the light and the noise. All his friends are terribly pleased to see us. Someone presses a glass into my hand, a plate of food, I dance with one, and then another, but always he comes back to claim me. Then the music turns slow and dreamy, and after a while he leads me upstairs to a room with a great four-poster bed all hung with black velvet, and I find out what I have been missing all these years. I don't know if the earth moved, but that bed certainly did. I went to sleep in his arms . . .

And woke up on a cold bench in the town centre. Six o'clock in the morning. I'm stiff as a board, freezing, my head aches, and there is a strange hollow emptiness inside me.

I caught the first bus home. Vince was in bed, snoring. I told him I'd stayed over at my sister's. I knew he'd never bother to check. Funny thing is, we seem to get on better now, since it happened. Maybe I appreciate him more. Alright, I know he's a slob, but his heart's in the right place.

I've got to find that house. Maybe his friends will tell me where he's gone, if they're still there. Only it could be anywhere. I never noticed which way the car was going. And I didn't even catch his name properly. Something foreign. He said he was over on business, and when I asked what sort he smiled and said 'Stealing hearts.' I laughed, I didn't know what he meant.

I do now, of course.

It's not fair, he can't just leave me like this. What if I had to go into hospital or something? They'd be bound to notice, and then where'd I be? I want it back. Or at least a replacement. I thought I'd found a clue the other day. There was this bit in the evening paper, tucked away at the bottom of the page.

Police are puzzled by the discovery, it said, *in a doorway in Wolverhampton town centre, of a cardboard box containing a human heart.*

Nothing about what they'd done with it. I don't know. It might not even be the right one. The paper never said if it was still beating.

You think they'd have mentioned that.

Surely?

Thunderguts in Love

Thunderguts the troll lived in a deep dark cave under the mountain. It was a commodious residence, with all the traditional conveniences - damp walls, muddy floor, cold running water straight through the middle - and travelers along the nearby high road provided a steady food supply. He should have had everything a troll could desire, but he was not happy. He was lonely.

He wanted to meet a lady troll, but there were none nearby. He did hear of one unattached female living beyond the mountains, and set out to find her. After a long and arduous journey he arrived, only to discover she had been snapped up the week before by a passing ogre. He returned disconsolate.

Then he saw an ad in the personal column of 'The Bogle'. It was for 'Trolling Around - an Introduction Service for Lonely Trolls'. What have I got to lose? he thought. So he sent off his details and photo, plus a large fee, and settled down to wait.

Six weeks later came a knock at the cave door. Outside stood a small female troll. Thunderguts gaped in amazement, and fell in love on the spot.

'Hello,' she said. 'I'm Ethelene. This your cave? Not bad. When can I move in?'

'Now!' gasped Thunderguts.

She was his dream come true. She was nearly as broad as she was long. Her hair grew down to the bridge of her extremely long nose. Her eyes crossed invitingly, and her face was covered in the cutest little warts. To complete her charms, she exuded a strong and strangely alluring odour, especially from the feet. She was exquisite.

Ethelene soon took Thunderguts in hand. No longer could he lie around all day, waiting to grab any old passing traveler for dinner. She insisted on the best, so he had to go out and hunt for particularly fat and tender ones. Then she said the cave wasn't big enough, and had him excavate several more rooms. And she threw out his bone collection. The last straw came when she made him open up a hole in the roof, so she could take a shower when it rained.

'What's wrong with standing outside if you want to get wet?' he cried.

'It's uncivilized,' said Ethelene. 'Besides, you have to humour me. I'm expecting.'

'Expecting what?' said Thunderguts.

'Baby trolls, of course,' simpered Ethelene. 'Soon you'll hear the scamper of tiny hairy feet.'

It was too much. He did not feel ready for the responsibilities of fatherhood. And she might have asked him first, he thought. Early next morning he packed his favourite stone club and a haunch of smoked market consultant for his lunch, and crept out of the cave while she was still snoring. Thunderguts was nevermore seen in that vicinity. Some say he went to live under a motorway intersection, where he preyed on jack-knifed artics.

Ethelene and her brood live on in the cave, until the increasing mortality on that stretch of road caused the authorities to replace it with a bypass. After that they migrated to the nearest town, where they blended in with the populace, eventually becoming well established in both local government and organized crime.

Missionary

The alien was curled up on the doorstep when Daisy went to put out the empties. It was small and rotund, and covered in silky golden fur. Rather like a ginger cat, except for the eight legs.

'I come in peace,' it said.

'Would you like a saucer of milk?' said Daisy.

She wished she was more suitably dressed. It didn't seem right, receiving an intergalactic visitor wearing a dressing-gown and her old slippers.

'I wouldn't say no to a cuppa, if you're making one,' said the alien.

'You'd better come in then.'

The alien settled itself in the armchair by the fire while Daisy made tea and opened a packet of Garibaldi biscuits.

'I suppose you are wondering why I am here,' said the alien.

'I was a bit.'

'I am the representative of the Universal Mind.' it said, and sipped its tea though a tube which extruded from its body. It was surprisingly adept at manipulating the teacup, considering it had no fingers. 'I am here to spread Enlightenment.'

'Some sort of missionary, like?' Bugger, she thought. I'll never get rid of it now.

'Are you afraid of me?'

'No - should I be?'

'Of course not.'

Its voice murmured at the back of Daisy's mind. Funny how it could talk without a mouth. The scent of custard creams which emanated from it grew stronger, and Daisy felt herself relax.

'I have come to save Mankind. Your planet is heading for disaster, and your species for extinction. I bring you Fulfillment, Happiness and Peace.'

It slurped the last of its tea and held out the cup for a refill.

'We could do with a basin of that,' said Daisy. 'What took you so long?'

'The Universal Mind has watched you for countless eons as you groped your way out of the primeval slime, hoping you might gain the Higher Consciousness through your own efforts. It does not believe in interfering, except as a last resort. Only when a Dominant Species is facing imminent extinction is it prepared to intervene.'

'Goodness, that sounds serious.'

'It is. Your kind argues and fights within itself because its units cannot communicate with each other, mind to mind, as I am speaking to you. You are plagued by deceit and confusion. Once you attain true understanding, all this conflict will die away. But I cannot do this alone. I need your help.'

Here it comes, thought Daisy. Donation time. Well I'm not giving more than a quid.

'Me?' she said. 'You need to speak to the government about that sort of thing.'

'D'you thing we haven't tried?' said the alien. 'Ideally we need the permission of a World Government, but you don't have one. We have been sending missions here for years, only to me met with suspicion, even violence. Some managed to escape; others vanished without trace, with all news of their arrival suppressed. No, we have given up on governments. Even if we could get them to listen, there's no chance of them all agreeing.'

'What are you going to do, then?'

'In a real emergency, the consent of any member of the Dominant Life Form will suffice.' The alien took another swig of tea. 'You belong to the Dominant Life Form, yes?' it said.

'I suppose so,' said Daisy.

'Do we have your permission? Think carefully. The continued existence of your species, perhaps your whole planet, hangs on your reply.'

'I dunno,' Daisy hated this sort of decision. 'What have you got in mind?'

'I have brought an Intercelebral Communication Amplifier which, when fed into the system you call the 'Internet' will realign all your thought waves into one harmonious pattern. Mankind will become like my own people, plugged in to the Eternal Truth. All thoughts and desires will become known; lying will be impossible; deception and misunderstanding will vanish. What is more, it comes with direct access to the Universal Mind. Won't that be nice?'

'Hmmm. Is it safe?'

'Of course it's safe.' The alien's fur rippled and turned a deeper shade of orange. 'Adverse reactions are practically unknown.'

'Okay then, I'll give it a try. What do I have to do?'

'Lead me to your PC.'

'Don't have one,' said Daisy.

'Oh shit,' said the alien.

But it cheered up when Daisy told it there were some in the local library, and offered to take it there in the morning. She made up a nest for it in the spare bedroom and they both retired for the night.

Next day Daisy and the alien went to the library, where it was issued with a visitor's ticket and shown how to log on. The alien attached a small device to one of the UCP ports and downloaded a program. It only took a few minutes.

'I'll be off, then,' it said as they went outside. 'The program will activate tomorrow when the computers boot up.'

'Aren't you waiting to make sure it works?'

'Don't worry, it will work. I have to be out of range, in case my thought waves cause interference.'

'I see,' said Daisy. 'Well, it was nice meeting you.'

'Likewise, I'm sure,' said the alien. 'Thanks for the tea.'

Next morning Daisy woke up early. Bloody strange dream, that, she thought. She went downstairs and switched the telly on while she ate her breakfast.

' . . . extraordinary scenes in the House of Commons,' the newsreader was saying, ' when the Chancellor admitted that his entire monetary strategy of the past three years had been mistaken, and he hadn't the foggiest idea what to do next. He then burst into tears and was led out of the Chamber. . . '

Daisy switched off. Political stuff bored her silly. She chomped her toast, then took her rubbish out to the bin. Next Door was hanging out the washing

'Morning Mrs Bodger, how are you today?' said Daisy.

'Ooh, dreadful,' said Mrs Bodger, 'I've been up and down all night with my indigestion.'

'That's because you're stuffing your face all the time,' said Daisy. 'No wonder your stomach can't take it.'

Mrs Bodger turned puce and marched back into her house, slamming the door

What ever came over me, thought Daisy. The words were out of my mouth before I could stop them. She'll never lend me her drain clearer again.

Well, it couldn't be helped. Daisy decided to pull herself together and go and do her shopping. She fancied a nice bit of fish for her tea. As she walked down the road towards the shops, she heard running feet behind her.

'Help!' squeaked a terrified voice, as Mr Warble from over the way ran past, minus his trousers, closely followed by Mrs Warble clutching a meat cleaver.

Dear me, thought Daisy, I never knew Mabel Warble could run that fast.

On reaching the shop she chose a packet of breaded plaice from the freezer and took them to the counter. Now, she had always thought Cyril Wendover who kept the corner shop was an inoffensive sort of chap, but as he looked her in the eye her mind became flooded with the most extraordinary images, of her and him rolling around on some sort of fur rug, she could almost feel his hands crawling all over her . . .

'I'll have one of them custard tarts,' she said, faintly.

'That will be two seventy-eight. How about a quick shag behind the detergents?'

Daisy took her change and fled. When she reached home she switched on the telly again, then slumped at the kitchen table, gazing blankly at the screen, which was showing a riot at the United Nations, while the headlines flowed past on the strap-line at the bottom. The government had resigned. So had the opposition. Diplomatic relations had broken down all over the globe, and the value of all major currencies had plummeted. The Archbishop of Canterbury had walked out of a service, saying 'This is all a load of bollocks'. Not all the news was bad - the police had announced a much improved clear-up rate as sixty per cent of persons in custody had confessed (though not always to the crimes they were accused of). However, this was outweighed by the overnight rise in the murder rate, and fresh bodies were still being discovered.

Several wars had already broken out.

Bloody alien, thought Daisy. That's the trouble with these missionary types. They come in with their big ideas, promising to solve all your problems, and you end up worse than you were before.

It could have left me its phone number.

The alien, from its parking orbit around Jupiter, watched events on Earth unfold until the whole place went up in one massive thermonuclear bang.

Ah well, you win some, you lose some, it thought, and set course for Alpha Centauri.

A Pain in the Dragon

The Great Hall of the castle was shrouded in the darkness before dawn. The king's brave knights, worn out by a heavy day of jousting (followed by an even heavier night of carousing), were flat out under the banqueting table.

Suddenly a clear voice rang out. 'Get up, you lazy lot!'

Answer came there none, except for resounding snores.

'Come on,' repeated the voice, 'let's be having you – that dragon won't fight itself, you know.'

This was greeted by groans, and the occasional muttered 'Bugger off!'

'I heard that,' said Princess Dulcibella (for it was she).

Princess Dulcibella was taking her duties seriously. Left in charge of the kingdom while her father was off clobbering goblins, she was determined

78

to prove that she was perfectly capable of ruling the kingdom all by her, even though she was only a girl.

'I want to see you all washed, dressed and on parade in five minutes,' she said. 'If not – I have a cauldron of iced water here, and I am not afraid to use it.'

Ten minutes later Dulcibella was inspecting her troops on the parade ground. They were a sorry sight. The king had taken all his best knights with him to the Goblin War, and left her with the rejects. Not a single one of them had a complete, rust-free or undented suit of armour. Sir Halibert's visor kept falling down over his face all the time, Sir Willibrand's gorget was on the wrong way round, and Sir Humungeous had grown too fat to wear his armour at all, and appeared in a mail shirt and leggings. And they were the best of the bunch.

Dulcibella sighed. So much easier, she thought, to sit in her tower and wait for a prince to come to the rescue, but she was not prepared to be that sort of princess. It could not be helped. She would have to do her best with the materials to hand.

'Gallant knights,' she began, 'as you may have heard, last Wednesday a dragon alighted in the meadow by Bullocks Bottom. It has already eaten three pigs, two cows and a burgher, and severely singed the roof of the Parish Hall. This cannot go on! I propose, with your help, to ride out and slay the beast. Are you with me?'

There was a resounding silence, as the knights shuffled their feet and tried to avoid her eye.

'Oh, come on,' she urged. 'Killing dragons – that's what knights are for.'

'Can't it keep till the king gets back?' asked Sir Willibrand.

'There might be no kingdom to come back to, if we wait that long,' snapped Dulcibella. 'We must set out at once.'

'But we haven't had breakfast,' wailed Sir Humungeous. 'No-one fights dragons on an empty stomach.'

'Better to miss breakfast than *be* breakfast. We ride out at dawn.'

Shortly afterwards Dulcibella set out, leading her intrepid band of knights. She had put on her new designer armour, pleased to have a chance to wear it at last. It would not have protected against a well aimed pea-shooter, but it looked pretty.

It was not long before they began to see signs of the dragon's presence, in the shape of charred hedgerows and fleeing peasants.

'You don't want to go up there,' called a fat woman with a hen under each arm. 'It's not safe.'

'She's right, you know,' said Sir Halibert. 'We don't want to rush into this sort of thing. Why don't you call a conference, your Highness, and we can discuss it?'

'There's no time for talking,' said Dulcibella, 'we must press on.'

The came to a small wood, which had evidently suffered a forest fire and been reduced to blackened stumps. Smoke still shrouded it, from the midst of which came the sound of snoring.

'He's asleep,' whispered Dulcibella. 'We can creep up on him and get him before he wakes.'

So they crept up as quietly as they could, which was not very as knights can't help clanking, until the dragon lay before them. Dulcibella stood, her mouth hanging open. She had not expected him to be quite so *big*. For the first time she wondered whether her knights had been right. Perhaps this was not a terribly good idea.

The dragon opened one eye. 'Are you pudding?' it asked.

'I am not! I am the Princess Dulcibella.'

The dragon opened the other eye, taking in her regal bearing and shining armour. 'A princess – my favourite dessert. And tinned as well! I can keep you for later.'

It belched, and a gout of flame shot past them, catching the end of Sir Willibrand's moustache which flared up then shrivelled to nothing.

'Oh dear,' groaned the dragon. 'I should never have ate that burgher. I knew he was a bit off as soon as I'd swallowed him. He's disagreeing with me something dreadful.'

'I'm not surprised,' said Dulcibella. 'Most people disagree with being eaten. Serves you right if you've got indigestion.'

Then she had a brilliant idea. 'If I give you something to for it, will you go away and leave this kingdom alone?'

'Well, I dunno,' said the dragon. 'I like it here. Grub's good (if you keep off the burghers). And I get a princess thrown in.'

'The kingdom next door has seven princesses. I'm sure its king would be able to spare you one or two.'

'Hmmm – seven, you say?

'Fat ones.'

The dragon licked its lips, then winced at another spasm of dyspepsia. 'And you've got something will cure stomach-ache?'

'Certainly.'

'Okay, you're on.'

'Right,' said Dulcibella. 'Sir Halibert, would you mind galloping over to the village and fetching a large cauldron. I'll need it filled with water. And Sir Willibrand, please find the nearest apothecary and purchase a pound of bicarbonate of soda.'

When the ingredients came, she mixed them up. 'Here,' she told the dragon, 'drink this and you'll feel much better.'

The dragon bent its great head, and drank. It burped again, this time without the flames. 'Thanks awfully,' it said.

'Off you go then,' said Dulcibella.

The dragon flapped its wings and lumbered into the air. It circled them once, emitted a farewell belch, and was gone.

'Job done,' said Dulcibella, with satisfaction.

'Congratulations, Your Highness,' murmured the knights.

'Only one thing bothering me,' said Sir Humungeous. 'Isn't it a bit hard on next door's princesses? I thought they were friends of yours.'

'Oh,' said Dulcibella, 'I sort of forgot to mention that next door's king has seven sons as well. All of them renowned dragon killers. Now, let's go home. I want my breakfast. By the way, Sir Willibrand – sorry about your moustache.'

'Oh, it will grow again,' said Sir Willibrand. 'No lasting damage.'

Then Dulcibella and her gallant band returned to the castle, with crowds of peasants cheering them on their way.

If I never manage to nab a prince, she thought, I could always became a Dragon Control Operative.

Eggbound

The driver picked up his microphone and coughed.

'The company regrets that there will be a slight delay, due to there being a dead kangaroo on the bus.'

The passengers groaned.

'It's a bit much,' grumbled the fat lady in the green jodhpurs. 'First we got stuck behind those flying pigs in Aldershot - now this! Some of us want to get home tonight.'

'How come they let a kangaroo on in the first place?' demanded the dwarf with the false teeth. 'Did it have a ticket?'

'What I'd like to know,' said the off-duty detective, 'is – what did it die of?'

'I don't care,' said the fat lady, 'as long as it's not catching. Can't we dump it and get on?'

'I'm sorry, madam,' said the driver, 'but we have to go through the usual procedures. Was anyone accompanying the animal?'

The passengers avoided each other's eyes. No-one owned up.

'In that case, we have to stay put pending investigation. That's the regulations. I'm not licensed to transport the deceased, human or animal.'

'But how long will that take?' The fat lady began to cry.

'Perhaps I may be of assistance,' said the detective. 'I have had considerable experience in solving similar mysteries.'

He made his way to the back seat, where the marsupial corpse lay stretched out on its back, front paws held stiffly aloft.

'Let me see . . . aha!' He reached into the kangaroo's pocket and produced an egg. Holding it up, he looked solemnly round at the others.

'No-one must leave this bus. I suspect there has been – fowl play.'

From her perch on the luggage rack, Chicklit the hen watched with concern. She nudged her friend Eggwina.

'They've found the egg.'

'Oh no! We'll never get it back now.'

'It was a stupid idea, giving her one.'

'I was sorry for her. She looked a bit broody, I thought it would cheer her up. I didn't expect her to go off with it.'

'Shurrup!'

The detective was listening. 'Quiet, everyone. I think I hear – clucking.'

'Your clucking right you do,' cried Eggwina. 'Give me that that egg!'

With a fearsome cackle she swooped towards him, causing him to drop the egg. It cracked, and a small chick emerged.

'Precious!' cried Eggwina. 'Come to Mummy.'

'We seem to have a case of eggnapping,' said the detective. 'But have the hens committed kangacide?'

At that moment there was a load groan from the back of the bus. Everyone turned to see the kangaroo sitting up, clutching her head.

'Bounda, love,' shouted the dwarf. 'You're alive.'

'Are you with this kangaroo?'

'Yes. I didn't want to say, when we thought she was dead, but she was only sleeping off a bender. Oh, the relief.' He burst into tears.

'In that case, no crime has been committed and we can continue on our way.'

All the passengers cheered.

'Hang on,' said the driver. 'Has she paid? Because if not she can just hop off.'

The kangaroo reached into her pocket and produced a ticket.

'OK then.'

And they continued on their way.

All the little teddy bears

Once upon a time, deep in the country, there was a cottage with a thatched roof and roses growing round the door, and a little man living at the bottom of the garden. The little man was me, and still is for that matter. I've got an upturned flowerpot conversion behind the shed. The people in the cottage, Emily and her father, they don't bother me. He doesn't know I am here, and Emily - well, she's a friend.

I've known her ever since they came here, when she was four. It did not take her long to spot me. At that age they believe what they see. Not that it matters. If they tell no-one listens, and by the time they are ten or twelve they have stopped believing it themselves. Emily can still see me, though. She comes down most days for a chat, brings me a bit of something for my tea - cake maybe, or cheese. I'm very partial to cheese.

One afternoon I could see that she was upset, and after a little coaxing she told me what the matter was. Did I say that her mother had gone off years before, when she was still only a baby? Not that it seemed to bother her, and she adored her dad. Anyway, it turned out that he'd been seeing some woman for ages, keeping very quiet about it, and now he wanted to have her to stay 'so that they could get to know each other'. It looked like she might be getting a Stepmother, and we all know about them. No wonder the poor girl was worried.

'Has she got children of her own?' I asked.

'No. She collects teddy bears.'

That was a relief. Everyone knows the Wicked Stepmother is ten times worse if she has her own children.

I had my first sight of the Prospective Stepmother the following afternoon. She came tripping down the garden path, hanging onto Emily's dad's arm, all long skirt and trailing scarf, beads and trinkets, her hair piled up and coming down in wisps. I could hear her all the way down the garden, wittering away about ley lines and magnetic resonance and the powers of the earth spirits.

When she reached my end of the garden, which had been allowed to run to waste, she stopped and flung out her arms.

'I see water,' she intoned. 'A deep, clear pool with a willow weeping into it. A water garden!'

I did not like the sound of that for a start. Quite apart from the damp, pools mean goldfish and fish bring herons. I cannot abide herons. One took me for a frog once. It's not an experience I wish to repeat.

But worse was to come. She was going on about water elementals and I had stopped listening to her nonsense. I was trying to catch Emily's eye, she looked so miserable, poor child. I must have grown careless; the dock leaf I was hiding behind was not really big enough. The woman looked across - and saw me. She never so much as squeaked, just paused in what she was saying and smiled to herself, but I tell you, my blood ran cold.

Children, you see, I don't mind. If they babble about fairies no-one takes them seriously. And I enjoy the company. I get lonely, you see. There aren't many of us Little Folk around anymore. Of course they mustn't treat me like a doll (but no-one tries that twice!). Emily, bless her, has always been perfectly respectful, that's how we get on so well. No, children are all right, they only want to play, but adult mortals are quite a different matter. They want wealth and power. They want to use us and control us. When Emily came to find me after tea I had already almost finished my packing.

'What are you doing?'

'Leaving. I can't stay around here any more. That woman knows about me.'

'I know.' Emily flopped down onto the upturned wheelbarrow with no wheel, her usual seat. 'Dad must have told her. How could he? He knew it was a secret. All through tea she kept asking questions about you. She says she's writing a book. About fairies and such like, and how some of them are still around.'

This was worse than ever. I can cope with simple greed, but not a mortal out to prove a theory. Before I knew it I'd be in a cage with professors poking at me! I grabbed my bags.

'I'm off!''

'Don't leave me,' cried Emily in a panic. 'I haven't told her anything. I'll say you were just something I made up when I was little.'

'Too late for that. She saw me.'

'But I need you. I can't fight her on my own. She's ever so sweet on the surface, but I know she hates me really. I don't think she likes dad that much either. She's all over him, and then when he's not looking she switches off. Anyway, why should you have to move when you've been here so long, and you've got everything so nice?'

She had a point there. I was fond of my flowerpot. I'd got a proper fireplace with a chimney coming out of the hole at the top, and Emily had brought me some of her doll's house furniture. I would have a job finding somewhere else as comfortable. And

I've lived in this garden nigh on seven hundred years. I've grown attached to the place.

'We must get her to go away,' said Emily.

'It won't be easy,' I warned. 'She looks like she's got her hooks into your pa, good and proper.'

'Couldn't we use a wish?'

'Emily!'

Hadn't I warned her years ago about wishes? Didn't I tell her of the lad who wished for a barrow-load of gold and ended on the gallows because he never thought that folk would wonder how he came by it? Or the silly lass who wished to be beautiful to catch the lad she fancied, only squire took a fancy to her, and got her in no end of trouble. I don't know what it is with mortals and wishes. No good ever comes of them. You'd have thought they would have learned that by now. I made Emily promise, when she was just a little thing, never to ask.

'You can't just wish her away,' I told her, 'it would just make matters worse.'

'Then give her the wish,' said Emily.

I looked at her with respect. They call us tricky and devious, but I always say, if you want a really sneaky idea, go to a mortal. I never knew Emily had it in her.

'It might work. What's she doing tomorrow?'

'She wants to have a Teddy Bear's Picnic. It's her birthday, she says she's always had one on her birthday, since she was a little girl. She's brought the teddy bears with her, they're all over the front room. She talks about them all the time. She said that when she was little she used to believe that they came alive when she was not looking and played, like in the song. She used to try to catch them at it, but she never did.'

'Are you going?'

'She's asked me, but I don't want to. I think they're creepy.'

'Change your mind. Where's she having this do?'

'In the garden, I suppose.'

'I know a better place. You know the clearing in the middle of Hoggetts Wood? With the fairy ring?'

Emily nodded.

'Right. This is what you must do.'

Hoggetts Wood was a fair distance from the cottage, I had to set off before dawn to get there in time. I saw them coming over the fields, both clutching a great load of stuffed bears. Emily led the way into the heart of the wood. Once, troops of fairies had danced there on moonlit nights. All gone now. Only the great fairy ring was still there, and the ancient oaks around it.

The Stepmother was delighted with the place. She fluttered around setting up the teddies against roots and trunks, chattering away to them as she worked. A nasty looking lot they were too, all battered and decrepit. The one in pride of place had only one eye and one arm, and all its fur was missing. I had a word with Emily while the woman was preoccupied.

'Is it going to work?' she asked. 'She got really excited about the wish, but what if she's only pretending she believes me?'

I shrugged. 'Doesn't matter, as long as she uses the right words. And if she's really a good person, and means you no harm, then no harm will come to her. On the other hand - '

'What?'

'Well, wishes can be tricky things. I just hope we don't take out half the county. Listen. If it looks like turning nasty, and I shout 'Run!' don't wait to see why, just do it. Promise?'

She nodded.

The woman had finished fussing about. Now she was standing in the middle of the ring. Emily had told her what to say. You have to use the right words. It stands to reason. Mortals are always saying 'I wish this' or 'I wish that'. It would never do if one of us were to overhear and grant it. Could lead to some very embarrassing situations.

The Stepmother raised her arms.

'O fair and mighty Titania, I implore you, grant me my desire. I ask once, I ask twice, I ask thrice.'

Then she made her wish.

I think I can safely say that the teddy bears enjoyed their picnic. I was proud of Emily. When I shouted 'Run!' she never hesitated, she took off like a rocket, crashing through the bushes, making so much noise I'm sure she could not have heard anything. Well, I suppose she must have heard the screams, but not the snarls, the rending and crunching. It did not take very long. By the time help came there wasn't much left, and the teddies were the same as they had always been, except for the blood.

And is Emily living happily ever after? I hope so. They blamed wild dogs, or something escaped from a zoo, though nothing was reported missing. I don't think she remembers much about it,. though I can't be sure. She never comes to see me now, and if we meet in the garden her eyes just slide past me. It's only to be expected, she's growing up. Still, I miss her.

I could almost feel sorry for the Stepmother. She deserved it, of course; she must have been fairly vile for her wish to have turned out that badly. Still, I can't help remembering the look on her face as it was granted, the incredulous delight, then the dawning horror as they closed in and she saw the teeth.

Silly woman. You have to be very careful what you say when you make a wish. But who could have imagined anyone would have been stupid enough to want a picnic with real live bears?

They buried the teddies with her. Which I must say was a relief.

A Bit Off Colour

I remember well how it started. The rain had fallen all day, but it stopped as the sun was setting. I looked out of the window to see a beautiful rainbow, glowing with resplendent colours.

I'd seen plenty of rainbows before, but this one was different. Everyone says you can never reach the end of a rainbow, but I could see very well where this one ended. Right in the middle of our back yard.

I opened the back door and rushed out. I knew what you were supposed to find at the end of a rainbow, and if there were any pots of gold on offer I wanted my share. I half expected it to be gone, but it was still there. What's more, it looked very solid. I rapped on it with my knuckles and it felt like glass, not water vapour. I walked round it, staring. When I got to where the indigo blended into violet, I saw a door. Would this lead to the gold? Only one way to find out. I turned the handle.

Inside, a narrow flight of stairs led upwards, spiralling round the inner surface. I started to climb. Up and up I went till my knees were buckling. Just as I thought I could go no further, the steps flattened out as I reached the top of the arch. I was in a long arched hall, filled with glowing colours. I stopped to catch my breath.

'Good evening.'

I peered round, wondering who had spoken, as no-one was in sight.

'Who's there?'

'I suppose you've come about the job,' the voice went on.

'Job? What job?'

'Oh, caretaker, general maintenance. Painting, mostly. You have done some painting?'

'A bit of DIY,' I said. Too right I had. Redecorated the whole bloody house since I was made redundant. 'What's the pay?'

'Usual rates – crock of gold when you reach the end. And the job's half done already. The last bloke I had walked out. I don't know,' the voice sighed. 'You can't get the staff nowadays.'

Well, it wasn't what I was used to, but a job's a job.

'Okay,' I said. 'When do I start?'

'Right away. You'll find all you need waiting.'

I looked. Sure enough, a little way down the hall I could see an array of paint pots and brushes stacked on the floor.

'Just a minute,' I said. 'Who are you? And what about hours and meal breaks and days off and suchlike?

'I am the Management,' said the voice. 'Refreshment will be provided. What are 'days off'?'

Somehow it didn't seem worth making a fuss. I wasn't going to risk the only job I'd been offered in years. I went and picked up a paintbrush.

'I'll leave you to it, then,' said the voice.

It wasn't such a bad job. The Management provided meals at regular intervals, and plenty of tea breaks. When I got tired a bed would appear, and when I woke up there would be a Full English waiting. No, I couldn't complain about the grub. It was the boredom which got to me. Painting those stupid stripes. Red, orange, yellow etc. It got so I could have screamed from the tedium. I was lonely, too. No-one to talk to all day. The Management dropped by occasionally to see how I was getting on, but he/she/it hadn't much in the way of conversation.

That's why I did it, really. For a bit of variety. I didn't think anyone would notice.

I started out by playing around with the order of the colours. After all, it had been red through to violet from time immemorial. I reckoned we were due for a change. I started out by putting the green between the red and the orange. I liked the effect, so I tried the yellow between indigo and violet. Well, I thought it was an improvement. Then I painted red spots on the blue, and blue bands across the red. It definitely added interest.

I tried mixing my own colours too, but that wasn't a great success, I tended to end up with muddy browns and greys. Though I did manage some nice earth tones, and a really vibrant turquoise.

I must have been mad. Of course people noticed. I believe it caused quite a stir, with people thinking it meant the end of the world or such like. The scientific bods went bananas. I didn't mean any harm, and I said I was sorry. But Management was furious. Sacked me on the spot and slung me out. Never got a sniff of the gold, either. Said they were taking it to pay for the damage.

The worst of it was, the end of the rainbow wasn't in my back yard any more, it had moved on. Well, they do, don't they, rainbows. So I'm not to sure where I am, except it's a long way from home.

So I was wondering, could you spare a couple of quid? To help with the fare?

The feline conspiracy

From: *jason@wizard.co.uk*

To: *tanya@outline.com*

Subject*: Hi stranger*

Sent: *20 Feb 10:43:17*

Hi Tanya

How's the novel going? Finished it yet? Last I heard you'd hit a sticky patch in chapter nine. I'm thinking of binning mine by the way - it wasn't going anywhere.

I've started something new. I found this book at a boot sale the other day - one of those 'Mysteries of the Ancients, Gods from Outer Space' thingies - I thought it might come in useful. When you write fantasy you're always looking out for ideas. Well, it was fantasy all right, but not the honest, fictional kind. No, this was fantasy pretending to be fact.

I read it through in wonder and amazement. Did you know that the Knights Templars were really emissaries from an alien civilization? No, neither did I. There must be people who buy this drivel full-price. Someone published it. Someone got paid for writing it. For heaven's sake, they even made a TV series out of it.

So I've decided to give up fiction and write bollocks instead.

First, I needed a subject. It didn't matter how outlandish as long as it was original. That stumped me for a while. It's not easy finding something nobody else has done. Then the other night, while I was giving Tuck his tuna deluxe, it came to me.

The world is run by, and for the benefit of, cats.

It's perfect. It will appeal to the conspiracy theorists and the cat lovers. I shall call it 'The Feline Conspiracy'. It might even be true. Someone must be running the show, and I'm damn sure it's not us. It would explain that smug, all-knowing look they have. Take Friar Tuck, for example. I never *advertised* for a cat. He just walked in one day and took possession. He gets a roof over his head, three meals a day, unlimited tummy tickling, and what do I get? The dubious pleasure of his company.

I'll need to do some research, on Ancient Egypt, cat cults and so on, but I can start roughing out a proposal straight away.

Cheers

Jason

To: *tanya*

Sent: *3 April 19:36:40*

Sorry about your problems with Nefertiti. Still, you should find homes for the kittens easily enough. Tuck has been acting strangely as well. Normally he never takes any notice when I'm writing, but whenever I'm working on the book he won't leave me alone. He keeps jumping on my knee, rubbing his head against my face, dabbing at the keyboard with his paw. Sometimes he even sits on it. Very odd.

I've had a letter back from the publisher. He likes the idea, wants to see a synopsis and the first three chapters. I've done those already. At this rate I should be finished in a few weeks. Tuck permitting.

Be good

Jason

Sent: *11 June 15:12:23*

Hi Tanya

I heard your reading was a great success. Sorry I couldn't get to it, but I've been very busy.

The book is still going well. It's not difficult churning out this stuff. The basic technique is simple. You pick an undeniable fact, for example, that cats were sacred in Ancient Egypt. You then build some hypothesis on it - say, that the Egyptians recognised that cats were a superior species. Then you assume your hypothesis to be fact, and build another round of speculation on that . . . and so on. And on. You have to you keep saying you are going to prove this that and the other. If you repeat this often enough you can move straight on to 'as I have already shown' without anyone noticing that you have not actually proved anything. Include quotations from esoteric journals (you can make them up, no-one will check), or ancient manuscripts, now unfortunately lost. And don't forget to hint that the authorities know more than they are letting on. Remember the people who read this kind if thing are not very bright (if they were, they wouldn't be reading it).

Tuck is still being a nuisance. Last week he deleted three chapters. Good thing I save everything in the cloud. Then yesterday he chewed up five pages of hard copy and was sick all over the keyboard. If I believed what I was writing I'd be thinking sabotage.

Cheers

Jason

To: *Tanya@outline.com*

Sent: *19 July 08:17:51*

Great news! The publishers have written to say they want the complete manuscript as soon as possible. Apparently they have a gap in their list. That's really cheered me up, and I have to admit, I'm feeling a bit down this morning. I had this weird dream last night and I can't get it out of my head.

I dreamt I was lying in bed and Tuck was sitting on my chest breathing fish fumes into my face.

'Nyuggh!' I said.

'We wanted a word with you,' said Tuck.

At this point I noticed the room was full of cats.

'What?' I croaked.

'It's about this book you're writing. We want you to stop. It's too dangerous.'

'What do you mean - dangerous? It's only a bit of fun. It's not true.'

Silence.

'You can't mean – it's never - _'

'Not quite. Not exactly the way you've written it, but near enough.'

I would have laughed if there hadn't been several tons of cat squashing my diaphragm.

'But no-one's going to believe it!'

'And what if someone did? Every time one of you has found out about us, the result has been persecution. Have you any idea how many cats were slaughtered in the middle ages?'

'This is ridiculous,' I protested. 'I've put weeks of work into that book. I'm not going to give it up just because a load of moggies don't like it.'

I could sense tails twitching all around the room.

'I told you this was a stupid idea,' snapped the ginger tom from next door but one. 'You can't reason with monkeys.'

Tuck quelled him with a glance. 'Some of my friends wanted to proceed to extreme measures, but I managed to persuade them that a friendly warning would be enough for now. Just make sure you heed it.'

'And if I don't?'

A dozen pairs of green eyes glared at me with unmistakable menace.

'Sssteps will be taken,' hissed a Siamese.

Tuck rose and began to walk down my body, every paw sinking six inches into my stomach. At my groin he looked back.

'Be a good lad. Just drop it. All right?'

I sat up. 'What makes you think you're doing such a brilliant job running the world anyway,' I called after him. 'Perhaps it's time us monkeys had a go!'

I know it was only a dream but it's shaken me up a bit. It was so real. Still, enough of that. I must get on. I have a deadline to meet.

Jason

Sent: *28 August 18:43:07*

Well, I've finished the book at last. I must say, I am pleased with it, though it took me longer than I expected. I think it has exactly the right mix of plausibility and insanity. After reading it, no-one will look at a cat in quite the same way. Tuck has given up interfering. He's been very aloof lately. I hope I haven't offended him. He spends most of his time out hunting. He brings home dead mice all the time and leaves them around for me to find. There was a headless one on the keyboard this morning. Not funny.

Anyway, I'm done. The book is all printed out and parcelled up, ready to send out. I'll post it off in the morning. Tonight I'm going into town to get totally rat-arsed.

Sent: *August 29 06:14:22*

I found this weird message on the screen when I got back. I must have passed out, because the next thing I remember it was morning and I was lying on the floor with a splitting headache. The words were still there. I dragged myself to the desk and waited for my eyes to focus.

DRE JASON it said. YU SHOUD HAVE LISSEND. YOUU GOT IT ALL WRONG. ALL WEVE EVER DOBNE IS FIGHT YUR ENEMIS. I WARND YOU. TOO LATE NOW. YUOR PROTECTION HAS BEEN WITHDRAWN. SORRRY. TUCK

It wasn't there when I went out last night. Come to that, I left the computer switched off, I'm sure I did. I wish I could think straight. Cats don't leave messages on computers. Do they?

I'm losing touch with reality.

I want to throw up.

Sent: *August 29 06:23:15*

Dear God. I've seen them. They're out there, waiting for me. I opened the door and there they were, massing in the hall, bodies pressed together, a heaving grey horde with red eyes and naked pink tails. I slammed the door shut.

What did the message say? All we've ever done is fight your enemies.

Rats.

The real enemy. Cats have protected us from them throughout human history. Tuck, I'm sorry, I didn't understand. Come back. Please.

I can hear noises from the other side of the door; claws scrabbling, rodent teeth gnawing. How long will it take a few hundred rats to chew through a door?

Please, Tanya, help me. I left my phone in the kitchen. Call the Police. Call the Fire Brigade. Call Environmental Health.

For heaven's sake, look in your inbox.

HELP!

The little brass monkey

Once upon a time there was a little brass monkey. He lived with his friends, China Dog and Crystal Hedgehog, on a nice warm mantelpiece above the fire.

One morning Brass Monkey woke up, and the world outside the windows was different. Everything was white.

'What is it?' he cried.

China Dog, who was an antique and so had seen a few winters, said, 'It's called snow. It happens when the weather gets cold. All the children go out to play in it. They make snowmen, and throw snowballs, and slide on the ice.'

'That sounds fun,' said Little Brass Monkey. 'I want to go out and play.'

'You can't do that,' said Crystal Hedgehog. 'Don't you know what happens to brass monkeys who go out in the cold?'

'No. Do you?'

'Not exactly,' admitted Hedgehog. 'But,' she added in a whisper, 'I've heard it's something quite, quite dreadful.'

'I think you're making it up,' growled Brass Monkey. 'Are you coming?'

China Dog looked over the edge of the mantelpiece and shuddered. 'We can't climb down there,' he said. 'What if we slipped? We'd break.'

'Suit yourself.' Brass Monkey jumped from the mantelpiece, bounced three times on the hearthrug and stood up.

'Are you all right?' called Hedgehog.

'Not a dent on me.'

Little Brass Monkey ran to the window, and began to climb up the curtain. The small window at the top was slightly open. He squeezed through and dropped down into the snow.

What fun he had! He threw snowballs the size of peas at the children, but they never noticed. He slid on their slide. Wheeee! It was cold, but he ran around to keep warm.

He bumped into a snowman.

'What are you doing out here?' asked the snowman. 'Don't you know brass monkeys should stay where it's warm, if they don't want to risk losing their -

'

'Bollocks!' said Little Brass Monkey.

'Exactly.' said the snowman.

'You can't scare me!' cried Monkey, and ran off again.

But it was starting to get dark in the garden, and the children had gone in for their tea. Perhaps it is time I went back inside, thought Little Brass Monkey.

Only when he went back to the window, there was no curtain on the outside for him to climb up, and the wall was slick with ice. He went to the back door, but it was shut tight.

He crouched on the step, shivering. It grew colder and colder. After a while he could not feel himself at all. Not his hands nor his feet, not his tail or . . . anything. It was a very long night.

Eventually the sun heaved itself over the horizon, touching the snow with pink. The house began to stir. The door opened.

'What's this? Our brass monkey? Who took him outside?'

Someone picked him up and carried him inside, while two tiny brass spheres gleamed unnoticed in the morning sun, soon to be kicked off the step to disappear into the snow.

Little Brass Monkey sat and shivered so hard the whole mantelpiece vibrated. It was a long time before he thawed out enough to answer the enquiries of his friends.

'What happened to me? I got locked out, that's what happened,' he squeaked at last.

'Your voice sounds strange,' said Crystal Hedgehog.

'I think,' said China Dog, 'you've lost something.'

Little Brass Monkey looked down - and squealed a terrible squeal.

He recovered, up to a point, but he was never the monkey he had been. So the moral of this tale is - if you are a brass monkey, stay in the warm, or you too may go out a baritone and come back a countertenor.

The ice maiden

Prince Leon was the King's third son. It was, he considered, an unenviable position. The first son had it made; all he needed to do was keep his nose clean and wait for the top job to become vacant. Likewise the second son. He could get on with his life, while keeping himself in readiness in case number one dropped off his perch untimely. But the third son - people expected things of a third son. Leon was in favour of a quiet life, but he feared it was not to be.

He was right. The morning after his twenty-first birthday, still suffering from a hangover, he was summoned before the king and council.

'Well, my lad,' said the king. 'So now you're twenty-one. How time flies, seems like yesterday you were in nappies. Still, I'm sure you can't wait to be off on some Quest or other, slaying the odd dragon, rescuing princesses, finding yourself a nice little kingdom somewhere. I was just the same at your age.'

Prince Leon gulped. 'I don't suppose I could stay here and be a chartered accountant?'

The court gasped in horror and the king turned an alarming shade of purple. 'Don't be ridiculous! Have you no respect for tradition? Young people these days, no ambition, no get-up-and-go. You want to see a bit of the world. Get some of that fat off you. Be off, before I disown you. On yer bike!'

(He didn't actually say 'on yer bike' as bicycles had not been invented, but you get the gist.)

The Queen sniffled and wiped her eyes with a lace hanky. 'I've packed your winter underwear,' she

128

said, 'and a bottle of cod liver oil. Remember, always wash behind your ears, and don't speak to strange women.'

So the prince's fate was sealed. He saddled his trusty steed, said a tearful farewell to Mandy at the Blue Gryphon, and within the hour the city gates had closed behind him.

He clopped disconsolately along the high road, keeping his eyes peeled for any sign of a suitable Quest, preferably something easily completed so he could be back home before the weather changed. Nothing showed up. By nightfall he had reached the margins of the Forest. No inn or any other sign of habitation was in sight. He unloaded his horse and tied it to the nearest tree, ate a couple of biscuits saved from his packed lunch, rolled himself in his cloak and went to sleep.

Early next morning he awoke, stiff, hungry - and alone. His horse had managed to free itself and, like a sensible animal, had legged it back to the palace. On investigating his saddlebags, with a view to lightening the load, he discovered that the cod-liver oil had leaked over his thermal vests. He stuffed the lot down the nearest rabbit hole.

He went on his way until he came to a stream. A willow tree overhung it, and clinging to its branches, her toes inches from the rushing water, was an old woman.

'You would appear to be in need of assistance, madam,' said the prince.

He leant out, grabbed her collar, and hauled her to the bank.

'Thank you kindly, young sir,' she said. 'Anything I can do for you in return?'

'Oh, that's okay, I'd better be getting along. Mother told me not to speak to strange women.'

'Well, I'm about as strange as they come. Are you always going to do as your mother tells you?'

'Not necessarily,' said Leon.

'My cottage is just downstream. Come and have some breakfast.'

It was the mention of breakfast which clinched it. Not long after, Leon was sitting devouring a large plateful of bacon and eggs. As he ate, he gazed at his hostess. She was indeed strange. No more than three feet tall, hunchbacked, hook-nosed, warts all over her chin, one green eye and one brown, she had 'witch' written all over her (or to be exact, embroidered across the front of her dress).

'I suppose you're on a Quest,' she said.

'How did you guess?'

'Why else would a young prince be out wandering the countryside? Though you don't look the adventurous type.'

'I'm not,' said Leon. 'All I want is to get the horrible business over so I can go home. You wouldn't know of anything suitable?'

'Well ... there's an ogre been making a nuisance of himself, over Little Wilting way. Ten foot tall, three heads, nasty temper - ?'

Leon shuddered. 'I don't think that's quite me. Haven't you anything a bit less physical?'

'Hmm ... you could always have a bash at the Ice Maiden.'

'Come again?'

'Princess Vivica. Only daughter of the late King Baldwin of Allopecia. Magically frozen into a block of ice by her wicked stepmother. Anyone who thaws her out gets to marry her.'

'That sounds more promising. Whereabouts is she?'

'In a castle about thirty miles north of here.'

Leon's face fell. Walking was not one of his favourite pastimes.

'I'll need a horse then. And a flame-thrower.'

'Oh, I think we can do better than that.'

The old woman began to rummage in various drawers and cupboards, muttering 'Now where . . . can't be far away . . . saw it just the other day . . . Ah!' She turned, brandishing a small wooden box. 'Here we are, the very thing.'

'What is it?'

'Inside this special magically flame-proofed container we have a genuine phoenix feather, on a chain. Pick up the feather by its chain (using the tongs included, and taking care not to touch it yourself or you'll be be chargrilled) hang it round the neck of the frozen princess, and she will melt on the spot. Guaranteed.'

'How much?' asked Prince Leon.

'No charge.' The old woman bared all three of her teeth. 'Virtue is its own reward. When I think of that poor young princess . . . In fact, to save time, you can borrow my broomstick. It will drop you by the castle.'

Leon would have preferred an hour or two to digest his breakfast (he hated to be rushed), but at the same time he could take a hint.

'Thank you, much obliged, you've been most kind.'

'Not at all.' She smiled again, sending a shiver down Leon's spine. 'After all, I owe you.'

Prince Leon swam to the edge of the moat and dragged himself up the bank.. The broomstick had taken the instruction 'Drop him off' rather too literally for his liking. The castle walls loomed over him. A drawbridge led to a gatehouse defended by a portcullis and a heavy iron-studded door. Pity the broomstick hadn't had the sense to drop him inside the castle. Well, no help for it. He squared his shoulders, took a deep breathe, squelched across the drawbridge and rang the bell.

After several minutes he heard footsteps and a window opened in the door.

'Yers?'

'Will you inform the Princess Vivica that Prince Leon of Lugubria would like to call on her?'

'Princess in't seeing no-one.' The window started to close.

'No, wait! Is - is the Queen receiving visitors?'

'I'll 'ave ter arsk.'

The window slammed shut.

Time passed. Prince Leon dripped. He hoped he did not have a cold coming on. At last the door creaked open and a varlet grudgingly motioned him inside.

''Er Majesty Queen Floribunda will see you now. Up the stairs, first on your right.'

Leon pushed open a door into what was obviously the Queen's private sitting room; he had the general impression of plenty of gilt, and mirrors, and plaster cherubs.

'Prince Leon? You're very welcome - why, whatever happened to you?'

She was not quite what he had expected. He'd thought the Wicked Stepmother would be something like the old witch (only a bit younger), not small and blonde and not much older than he was.

'Oh - er - had a bit of a mishap on the way - lost my horse - ' He sneezed.

'Oh you poor thing!' Her blue eyes widened in sympathy. 'You must have a hot bath *immediately.*' She tugged a bell-pull. 'I'll get them to find you some dry clothes.'

Some time later, bathed and wearing one of the late King Alphonse's second-best suits, he joined the Queen for dinner.

'I had hoped to meet Princess Vivica,' he said.

'Vivica won't be coming down this evening. She - she has a very bad cold. You'll have to make do with poor little me.'

Leon found this no great hardship. Queen Floribunda listened with admiration to all he said, laughed at his jokes - even the one about the toad and the commode, which no-one else had found funny, even after he'd explained it - and generally made him feel appreciated as never before.

'You will stay the night, of course?' she murmured.

It was difficult to remember that she was an evil witch who had cast a spell over a young and innocent girl. Perhaps the old woman had got it wrong and Princess Vivica *was* just suffering from a cold?

'Thanks. Most kind.'

Most useful. That night, after the denizens of the castle had gone to bed, Prince Leon pulled a fur-lined robe over his night-shirt and stuck his feet in a pair of borrowed slippers. Clutching the box with the phoenix feather in one hand and his candle in the other, he set out to discover the truth.

He wandered up and down staircases and along endless corridors, not sure what he was looking for or how he would know when he found it. At last as he entered one passage, he noticed a sudden drop in temperature. The further he went the colder it grew. His breath misted, and he began to regret ditching his thermal underwear. Then he saw it: the door at the end of the passage, white with frost.

A blast of cold air blew out his candle as he pushed the door open, but the room beyond was filled with moonlight. Frost furred the carpet and bedspread, icicles hung from the chandelier, and even the flames in the fireplace were blue. In the centre stood a white figure, a young girl carved in ice.

Leon stepped inside. The intense cold seared him, as with numbed fingers he fumbled with the catch on the box. He could scarcely pick up the tongs to take out the precious feather. It glowed red-gold on its chain, its warmth giving some protection against the chill, although he still felt certain portions of his anatomy were in danger of freezing solid and dropping off. With a supreme effort he forced himself near enough to drop the chain over the head of the statue.

As soon as the magic feather touched her things started to happen. The fire in the grate turned red, the carpet grew soggy as the frost melted, and he had to step back to avoid icicles falling like spears. The white figure began to be suffused with colour. Her dress became purple, her cheeks pink and her hair bright red. In a few minutes she was fully thawed, standing in a puddle of melt water, glaring around her.

'Who are you, and what do you think you're doing in my bedroom?' she snapped. 'And why is everything wet?'

'Er - I rescued you,' said Leon. 'Broke the spell. Ice. Remember?'

Princess Vivica blinked. 'Yes, it's coming back to me. It was all that cow Floribunda's fault. Right, I'll settle her. *Florrie!*'

She flung open the door and started down the corridor, Leon at her heels.

'I say, wouldn't it be better to wait till morning, when we've all calmed down . . . '

'FLORRIE!'

Doors were opening, people coming out to see what was going on. By the time they reached the Queen's apartments they had collected a sizeable crowd. Queen Floribunda emerged, clad in a pink silk negligee trimmed with ostrich feathers.

'Vivica! You've recovered, how splendid. '

'Guards! Throw that woman in the dungeon!'

A number of large men in the crowd hesitated.

'Who's King Baldwin's heir and your rightful queen? Her or me?'

The crowd shifted its feet uncomfortably. 'You, I suppose,' someone muttered at last.

'Then *take her away!*'

'Isn't that a bit harsh?' said Leon, as Floribunda was dragged away, squealing piteously.

'Is it? Thanks to her I've just spent eighteen months as an ice statue, and it was *freezing.* Well, I shall enjoy thinking up some suitable fate for her. Something lingering and painful.'

Leon followed her into the Queen's bedroom.

'Hang on - aren't you supposed to sweet and kind and forgiving?'

'Whatever gave you that idea?'

'I suppose I just assumed . . . '

'Well, don't. Who are you anyway?'

'Prince Leon, third son of the King of Lugubria.'

'Third son! I might have known. Get put under a spell, and you're sure to be stuck with some nonentity. And to think, before my indisposition, I was all set to marry an Emperor! Well, you'll have to do, though I would have preferred someone better looking. If you smarten up a bit and lose some weight . . . I don't suppose you have any money?'

'I have a Diploma in Theoretical Economy,' said Leon. 'But don't worry, I'll be off in the morning.'

'Off? What do you mean, off?' The Princess's voice rose. 'You have to marry me. It's in the rules.'

'I don't think we're suited. Perhaps your Emperor will still be available?'

'You're jilting me! You can't do that. Guards! Guards! Take this scurvy varlet to the dungeon.

So Leon spent the rest of the night comforting Queen Floribunda.

'I'm so scared,' she sobbed. 'Vivica's bound to think up something really nasty to do to me, she always hated me for marrying her Pa. She was a horrible child, and it's entirely her own fault she got frozen. If she hadn't tried to put that spell on me - '

'You mean it was her spell?'

'Yes. Her witchy godmother gave it her.'

143

'Ah,' said Leon. 'Old lady, hump back, warts? I believe I may have met her.'

'Luckily I was wearing a Reflective Charm, and it bounced back on her. Served her right! But she'll take it out on me now.'

'There, there. I'm sure we'll think of something.'

But nothing occurred, and in the morning they were dragged out in chains. The castle was filled with servants scurrying about, all with nervous and harassed expressions, and Vivica could be heard shouting in the distance.

She was waiting for them in the Throne Room, a smile of fiendish anticipation on her lips.

'Ah, the prisoners for sentencing,' she cried with relish.

'Wait a minute,' said Leon. 'Aren't you supposed to have a trial first?'

The Princess shrugged. 'Trial, sentence –
whatever. Now, I've thought of something really
amusing. Dearest Stepmother, how would you like to
wear my feather?'

Floribunda turned deathly pale. 'No, no! It'll
burn me up!'

'Look, if you let Florrie off,' said Leon nobly, '
I'll - I'll marry you after all.'

'You? I wouldn't marry you if you were the last
man on earth. I shall have you disembowelled and
staked out for the crows, as a warning to my other
suitors.'

'Kind of you to warn them off,' muttered Leon.

Vivica was not listening. She took the phoenix
feather from round her neck, and holding it by the
chain, moved towards Floribunda. But as she advanced,
something strange began to happen. Her steps slowed,
her movements became stiff, frost bloomed on her hair.

Panicking, she tried to replace the chain round her neck, but her arms would not move.

'Help me!' she gasped. 'I'm freezing!'

'Sorry, love,' said Leon, 'but I'm a bit tied up at the moment.'

A little later Leon was finishing breakfast in Floribunda's private sitting room.

'I'd better be getting along, now.' he said.

'Yes, you must have some awfully important things to do. Dragons to fight and such like. Princesses to rescue. I mean, stepmothers don't count.'

'Oh. Well. I suppose I'm not in that much of a hurry.'

Floribunda smiled. 'More toast?'

'Look, I know I'm only a third son, not much of a catch, but if you'd like me to stick around for a bit - '

'That would be very nice.'

146

After a while Floribunda lifted her head from his shoulder and enquired, 'What shall we do about Vivica?'

'Oh, I think we'll just - keep her on ice?'

Midnight Call

OWWOOooooh!

I climbed out of a deep pit of nightmare to find waking was worse. Thick night closed around me, smothering. The darkness was absolute. Only that ghastly cry resounded in my ears. Had it been part of my dream?

I dreamt I escaped across burning sands, the colour and consistency of congealing custard. The very air had seemed to solidify around me. I heard the scrabbling feet of the pursuing demons, felt their hot breath on the back of my neck . . .

As my eyes grew used to the darkness I could see the pale square of the window, clouds scudding across a gibbous moon. Slowly my breathing calmed, my pounding heartbeat quietened. I listened till my ears ached. All was silent.

There it came again! The hideous, wailing cry, of a soul wracked beyond endurance. The hair stirred on my head as I sat up, clutching the blankets around me. It had sounded so near, almost as if it was in the same house. I shuddered, fearing the infernal entities had escaped from my dreams to walk the earth. Perhaps one was even now approaching up the stairs.

Then I heard it. A soft, surreptitious scratching at my bedroom door. For a moment terror held me paralyzed, but I could not help myself. Some external force seemed to propel me from my bed and across the floor. I had to see.

My hand shook as I opened the door. It was there, its eyes blazing into mine, a headless corpse at its feet. I screamed.

'Bloody hell, Shagpile. I know you mean well and you're a brilliant hunter but - *I don't want your mouse!*'

Only he looked so disappointed I ate it anyway.

Silver Wolf

He woke and stretched, front legs first, then back, luxuriating in his strength. When every muscle was ready for action, he padded to the entrance of the den. Behind him the pack was stirring, although the winter dawn was still some time away. He paused at the entrance, muzzle raised, testing the air. More snow on the way. He remained still, his nostrils flaring as he sampled the varied scents born on the wind - of trees and growing things waiting under the snow, smoke

151

smells, man smells, and most interesting, smells which indicated the presence of his own kind. A rival barked in the distance, too far away to be a threat. He answered.

The world was black and silver, lit by a setting moon. His territory waited for him. It was time to visit his marks, checking each one to see if there had been any visitors since his last call. At each one he raised his leg to obliterate any alien scent, finishing by cocking it as high as he could, so that his mark would be highest. Any stranger passing through would think better of challenging him. Satisfied, he went on his way.

It was time to hunt. Not for large prey - but for something he might tackle on his own, a rabbit or a vole. He pressed on, every sense alert, until he caught a whiff of something interesting. Rat! He followed the trail eagerly, salivating already, only to stop as he detected a musky, feline odour. A big cat could be a formidable adversary. He would win, but the victory might not be worth the cost. Reluctantly he abandoned the chase.

He was passing, ghostlike, through a belt of trees when he stiffened, head raised, searching the air. There it came again. A strange female! He started across the snow, running now with a new sense of purpose. There it came again; she was nearby, waiting for him. He saw her - but stopped, abashed. She was not alone. Her own pack was ranged around her, protectively. They were too strong, too numerous, and he was alone. He could not challenge them. His tail drooped as he turned back, following his own track to safety.

His own pack would be waiting; he had left them too long. He hated to return without something to show for his efforts, but he could not always have a successful hunt. Another time, perhaps. First he must reassure himself that no harm had come to them while he was away.

Then, as he had almost given up hope, he caught the scent of food. An old kill, not very fresh but better than nothing. He grabbed a piece and dragged it to the den, laying his offering proudly on the floor.

'Eurch! Get that horrible old bone out of here! Where have you been you, bad dog? Don't you go jumping up at me! Down!'

The Silver Wolf wagged his tail, and went to get his breakfast.

The wishfish

Doris dumped her shopping bag on the kitchen floor and untied the strings of her rain hood. Dreadful weather, they'd had no summer at all. And her knee was playing up again. She lit the gas under the kettle and began to put away the shopping, leaving the kipper for Alf's tea out on the table.

She did not care for kippers herself, they repeated on her, but Alf was very partial to them. Had to be the real thing, mind, with their heads and tails still on, none of that boil-in-the-bag rubbish. She stared down at it morosely. The kipper stared back.

'Don't eat me,' it said.

'Pardon?' said Doris.

'I can grant wishes,' it went on eagerly. 'Health. Wealth. Power. Anything you like. Only not if you eat me.'

Doris sat down heavily, the kitchen chair creaking beneath her weight. 'Fish don't talk,' she said.

'I do,' said the kipper. 'I'm magic. Ever hear the story about the fisherman and his wife?'

Doris shook her head.

'He was dirt poor till one day he caught a magic fish in his net. It gave him everything he asked for, until his wife got too greedy . . . I was that fish.'

'But you can't be the same one,' protested Doris. 'I mean . . . '

'I'm immortal, aren't I? Must be,' it added glumly, 'to survive kippering. But I won't survive eating. So what do you say?'

'What about Alf's tea?'

'Give him something else! Think. You could have everything you ever dreamed of.'

The kettle was boiling away, unnoticed. Doris got up and made the tea. Anything she wanted! She didn't know where to start. That dress in Overdale's window, a new stair carpet, the bathroom window fixed . . . nothing seemed quite important enough.

'I could do him egg and chips, I suppose,' she said.

'That's the spirit!' said the kipper. 'What'll it be?'

Doris brought her tea back to the table. Her feet were killing her, and she was sure her ankles were swelling. Everything hurt.

'I wish . . . I wish I was young again,' she said slowly. 'And beautiful,' she added for good measure.

'No problem,' said the kipper.

It was a most extraordinary feeling. All her aches and pains drained away, leaving her feeling strangely light. She jumped from her chair and raced upstairs, clutching the waistband of her skirt to stop it falling down. She had to see what she looked like!

A vision stared back at her from the mirror. Herself forty years younger, but not as she had ever been. Her hair had never been so thick and glossy. Her face was still her face, just about, but its planes and proportions had been subtly altered.

She was gorgeous. Wait till Alf saw her!

He'd be back soon. She never let him in before four o'clock. He may be retired but that didn't mean she wanted him under her feet all day. Heavens! The kipper! He mustn't see that. She flew downstairs and had just stowed it safely away in the freezer when she heard his key in the door.

Alf's expression when he walked into the kitchen was everything she could have wished. His jaw dropped, his eyes bulged, and he had to take several deep breaths before he could speak.

'Who the hell are you?' he said.

Unfortunately it proved impossible to get Alf to accept that she really was Doris. The more she insisted, the more he fixed her with a blank stare and replied, 'No, you're not.'

That was Alf all over. Once he got an idea in his head nothing would shift it. Bedtime was the worst. No sooner had she settled in her half of the bed when he came shuffling in with his teeth in a glass, saw her, and yelped, 'Get out!'

Well, no-one was going to turf Doris out of the bed she'd slept in all her married life. But there was no way she could persuade him to join her.

'I daren't, I daren't,' he whimpered. 'What if Doris comes back? She'll kill me.'

In the end Doris gave him a couple of blankets and sent him downstairs to sleep on the sofa.

She decided she had made a fundamental mistake. She should not have tried to change herself without changing Alf as well. Next morning, after feeding him his breakfast and pushing him out of the door, she went back to the freezer for the kipper.

It was a bit stiff and unbending at first, but after she'd thawed it out it became quite amenable.

'Thought you'd be back. Old man not up to scratch?' it sniggered. 'Another spot of rejuvenation wanted?'

'Not exactly,' said Doris.

She'd been thinking about Alf, remembering him as a young man. He didn't seem quite good enough for the new her. She'd never really thought he was good enough for the old her, come to that.

'I was thinking, maybe, something a bit different, more caring and considerate. Romantic. And good-looking of course,'

'Humph. Don't want much, do you?'

'Of course, if it's too difficult . . . '

'Nothing is too difficult for Me,' said the kipper. 'Consider it done.'

That afternoon at four she heard the key as usual but instead of Alf in walked the most gorgeous man she had ever seen. Tall and slim, yet well muscled, with dark curly hair and melting brown eyes, he was all her dreams come true. He swept her into his arms.

'My darling,' he murmured in her ear.

'I've got your tea ready,' she stammered.

'Tea? Who cares about tea? It's you I hunger for.'

He led her, unresisting, up the stairs.

Doris settled down to her new life. She started calling herself Estelle. After all, she thought, if Alf couldn't believe I'm really Doris it's not likely anyone else will, and I never liked the name anyway. The new Alf she renamed 'Mario', after a film-star she'd once liked. He was very attentive, always bringing her flowers and little gifts, and taking her out to dinner in expensive restaurants.

She had one nasty moment when the hole-in-the-wall refused her card. Insufficient funds, it said. But she asked the fish for more money, and a suitcase stuffed with used fifties duly materialised under the bed.

She told people that Alf and Doris had gone to Australia, and she was a niece, looking after the house till they came back. She knew there was talk. A deathly silence would fall whenever she walked into the greengrocer's, and every time she went in the back garden Next Door would be peering over the fence, asking had she heard from Doris, and when were they coming back? Nosy cow.

Then one day the doorbell rang and there on the step was Alf's sister Gertie, all the way from Doncaster. Come to snoop, of course, though goodness knows how she found out. They hadn't spoken since the unpleasantness over the walnut-veneered wardrobe when Alf's mother died.

Doris trotted out the Austalia story, but she could see Gertie didn't buy it.

'Niece? Doris always said she had no brothers or sisters.'

'They didn't get on.'

She got rid of Gertie eventually, but she had a feeling she had not heard the last of her.

Doris sighed. She was tired of all this hassle. What she needed was a holiday. And why not? See the world. She'd often fancied going abroad, but Alf wouldn't fly and she got sick in a rowboat on the pond, so they'd always ended up in Skegness. She would go straight down to the travel agent's and buy two tickets to the most exciting place she could find!

Doris let herself into the house, stepping over the pile of bills and junk mail on the mat. It was good to be home. Not that she hadn't had a marvellous time, at least at first. They'd visited all the places she had only seen in films: New York, Miami, Disneyworld. Till Mario ran off with a lap-dancer in Acapulco. Took what was left of the money with him, the toad. Left her with her return ticket and barely enough to get home. Still, plenty more where he came from. And as for money, she only had to ask the kipper for another lot. But first, a nice cup of tea.

There was a funny smell in the house. Doris opened the back door to air the place, and - what a surprise! - there was Next Door hanging over the fence.

'Had a good time, dear? Glad I spotted you – '

I bet you are, thought Doris.

' - because I think you ought to know,' went on Next Door with barely concealed satisfaction, 'the police have been round. Asking ever so many questions, they were, about Doris and Alf. Still, now you're home you can sort it out. Give them your uncle's address in Australia. You have got it, haven't you?'

'Of course,' said Doris, fighting down panic.

The police! They would find out she had been lying; but what could she possibly tell them, that they would believe? Then like a light coming on in her brain, an idea came to her. She nearly laughed aloud in her relief.

All she had to do was go to the kipper, and wish that everyone would believe whatever she said. Then she could tell them what she liked. Even the truth. Why not the truth? She (and the kipper) would be famous. She might even get on the telly.

She had better get the kipper thawed out ready, she did not know how much time she had. She went into the scullery, opened the freezer -

And screamed.

The stench was appalling. Doris stared for a moment at the putrid mass of rotting food, then collapsed onto a chair. Too late she remembered the envelopes marked Final Demand on the mat. She must have forgotten to pay the electric before they went away!

How could she have been so stupid? She buried her face in her hands, barely able to comprehend her loss. No Mario. No money. No story.

No fish.

Steeling herself against the smell, she began to poke around among the debris, hoping against hope that something of the fish might have survived. She found it at last, but as she took it out of its bag it disintegrated into a formless, almost liquid mass from which one eye gazed mournfully back at her. Shuddering, she flung the kipper into the bin and scrubbed the smell off her wrinkled fingers.

Wrinkled?

The stairs were steeper than she remembered, and her clothes felt so tight she could hardly breathe. Fearfully she looked in the mirror. Yes, it was true; the old Doris was back.

She collapsed onto the bed. The spell must have ended when the kipper fell to bits, she thought. Well, it was fun while it lasted, and at least I won't have to worry about the police any more. I suppose Mario's turned back into Alf, as well. She thought of Alf in Acapulco, with the lap-dancer, and a slow smile spread over her face. The smile grew into a chuckle and then a laugh. She lay on the bed laughing until the tears came to her eyes, and in that moment she looked almost young again.

Moon Music

Sid wobbled along the road, voice lifted in song. He had enjoyed a splendid evening: the beer had flowed like – like beer, the company had admired his wit and wisdom, even Mabel the barmaid had ventured to crack a smile. Sid was at peace with the world, even if not all the world was at peace with him. As he passed the last cottage its window was flung up and a voice shouted, 'Shurrup you pillock, we're trying to sleep here.'

Sid took no notice. Some people just didn't appreciate music. 'Shine on, harvest . . . boon . . . croon? Ah, yes – spoon,' he warbled.

He wished the road would keep still. It had no business shifting around all the time. He paused by the gate into a field. Perhaps he should have a bit of a lie down, till the world sorted itself out.

He lay on his back in the stubble, staring up at the moon. The moon stared back. It had a face. No, really. Not like the one's you see in kids' picture book. A real face. Didn't look too friendly, either.

'What d'you think you're doing there,' said the moon. 'Haven't you got a home to go to?'

Sid thought for a moment. 'No,' he said.

He did have a home, of course, but he did not particularly want to go there. Mona would be waiting up for him (he wished she wouldn't, but she insisted), sitting there in her nightie and curlers, ready to start on him as soon as he got through the door.

'And what time do you call this? Some of us need our sleep you know, have to get up in the morning, not right keeping me up all hours, and don't say I could go to bed because I wouldn't feel safe leaving you to lock up, look at the state of you, no-one knows what I have to put up with, should have listened to my mother . . . '

No wonder her parents called her Moaner, she did nothing else but.

Sid smiled at the moon, his most ingratiating smile. 'I'd rather stay where I am, if you don't mind.'

'Suit yourself. But I ought to warn you – people who spend too much time in my company can end up a bit funny. Though in your case I don't suppose anyone will notice.'

Sid was no longer listening. He began to sing again. 'Shine on, shine on harvest moon, di dum di dum dum . . . '

'Will you stop that ghastly noise!' said the moon.

Sid broke off, affronted. 'My voice has been much – much . . . people like it.'

'Well, I don't. Why don't you listen to the real thing?'

'OK.'

Then, as he lay there, he heard the most beautiful music. It came from everywhere around him, the melody strange and yet somehow familiar.

'What is it?' he whispered.

'The waltz of the spheres,' said the moon, smiling. She was rather pretty when she smiled. 'Would you like to dance?'

'Yes, please,' said Sid.

The moon stepped down and took his hands, pulling him to his feet. They began to dance, stepping smoothly over the stubble field, up into the night air, whirling above the sleeping world, faster and faster, her light shining around him and through him, the exquisite, insistent melody filling his mind . . .

They found him next morning, lying in the field with a beatific smile on his face, babbling nonsense. They took him home to sleep it off, and when, after a couple of weeks, there was no change, to the local hospital. There he stays. His wife visits once a week for a ritual moan.

'He's happy, selfish pig. Doesn't care about me,' she grumbles. But he no longer hears her.

The ill-wind nail

Once upon a time there was a man. We'll call him Nigel. Now, Nigel was not a happy bunny. This was because he never had any luck. If he bought a raffle ticket, the number before or after it might win, but his never did. When he went on the works outing to the seaside, he was the one the seagull shat on. The only time he asked a girl out for a date his bus never turned up, and by the time he got there she'd gone.

This day he was feeling particularly miserable, because the firm he worked for had needed to make someone redundant, so they'd drawn lots to see who'd have to go - I don't need to spell it out. He was walking home along the canal towpath, passing the occasional fisherman hunched on the bank. He considered jumping into the canal. Only with his luck he'd land on one of the discarded shopping trolleys which lurked under the surface. Probably get blood poisoning.

The he noticed something on the ground in front of him, and bent to pick it up. It was a large iron nail, very ancient and rusty; except for the head, which had a curiously polished appearance. The nearest fisherman began straining at his line. For the first time in living memory, someone had caught a fish. Nigel ignored him. He brushed the loose dirt off the nail, then rubbed the shiny head on his sleeve.

As he did so two things happened. The fisherman was pulled unceremoniously from the bank, disappearing into the murky waters with scarcely a gurgle, and Nigel notice a fat leather wallet, lying in the long grass by the side of the towpath. It was stuffed with money.

From that moment on, Nigel's luck changed. There was an address in the wallet, and when he returned it (for Nigel was an honest man), the owner was so impressed he offered Nigel a job, at a far higher salary than his old one. Soon he had enough saved up to put down a deposit on a house, which he did just before house prices took off again. He started entering the competitions he found in newspapers or on the leaflets he picked up in supermarkets. He found that if he rubbed the head of the nail before he sent his entry in, he would win. In this way he acquired an expensive car, and took several holidays in exotic locations.

As time went on, though, he began to notice something strange. Every time he had some good luck, someone he knew, or was connected to him, or just happened to be standing near him at the time, had some bad luck. Their pipes burst, or their car was stolen, or they caught some unpleasant illness. Of course it had to be coincidence. It's an ill wind, he told himself. Anyway, he didn't really believe it was the nail that was responsible for his good luck. That was just superstition. All the same, he started to feel a little uneasy about using it. He put it away in a drawer.

Then he met Yvonne. She came to work in the office, and Nigel fell in love at first sight. So did she, but unfortunately not with Nigel. She only had eyes for the Head of Sales, Brent Youngblood. Brent was handsomer, richer and had a swankier car. Nigel hated him. He felt that if Brent was only out of the way … he could not have said when he first had the idea, it crept up on him. He resisted at first. Deliberately using the nail to bring someone bad luck seemed a touch immoral, even when it was a berk like Youngblood. On the other hand he was not the right man for Yvonne, surely it was Nigel's duty to save her? And this luck business was all nonsense anyway.

So Nigel found himself one day, skulking in one of the cubicles of the executive washrooms, the nail clutched in his hand. Brent came in, alone. It only took a moment to rub the nail head. A few days later Nigel came in to work to find Yvonne in tears, surrounded by female staff. Brent, on a business trip to Thailand, had been arrested with half a pound of heroin in his bag. Naturally he protested his innocence, but this did not wash with the Thais. Nigel reckoned he'd be out of the picture for at least twenty-five years.

Yvonne was now in need of comfort, which Nigel was happy to provide. The campaign to save Brent from the death sentence brought them together, and they soon became an item. Nigel was hopeful that she would agree to move in with him. One day, after a romantic dinner at his house, she happened to come across the nail.

'What on earth's this old thing?'

'Oh, that's my good luck piece.'

'How does it work? I know, I bet you rub - '

'No!' Nigel snatched it from her.

This led to a quarrel, and which she stormed of home in a huff. They soon made it up, but after this she would not leave the subject alone. She eventually winkled all the details out of him (except the business with Brent, of course). He didn't tell her about his suspicions of how the nail worked, either. He felt a bit guilty about that, as if he'd been stealing luck from other people.

She was always pestering him to give her a demonstration. Eventually he could stand it no longer. It was a roll-over week for the lottery, and the jackpot stood at twenty million.

'Go on,' she kept saying, 'why don't you? We could stop work, go away together. What are you afraid of?'

But he couldn't tell her. The argument grew more heated. In the end she said she was leaving forever, because he couldn't love her after all, and she didn't believe any of it, anyway.

'All right. ALL RIGHT' he shouted, and went to fetch the nail.

Later they sat watching the draw, the precious ticket in Yvonne's hand. When their numbers came up they hugged each other, laughing and crying, and Yvonne insisted on phoning up to claim immediately. Then they opened a bottle of champagne.

Nigel wanted her to stay the night, but she was worried about her cat and insisted on driving back to her own flat. He heard the news next morning. She had lost control on the bypass and hit a tree.

Nigel was devastated. He vowed never to use the nail again, but he could not bring himself to throw it away. He felt it was too dangerous: some other unsuspecting person might find it. Instead he wore it on a chain round his neck, as a perpetual reminder. The lottery win he left in the bank, untouched. He became deeply depressed, and eventually had to be hospitalised. There he was cared for by a nurse called Maureen. She was not as beautiful as Yvonne, but she had a lovely smile. As his depression gradually responded to modern treatment they fell in love, and when he was finally discharged they were married.

Their honeymoon was spent in the Italian Alps. One day, returning from an excursion in their hired car they were met by a wall of water. Rain in the mountains had sent a flash flood tearing down the valley. They climbed onto the roof of the car, but if was obvious the water was still rising.

Maureen clung to him. 'I'm glad,' she said, 'if we have to die, it will be together.'

Nigel felt the point of the nail digging into his skin. 'It doesn't have to be like that,' he said.

He drew out the nail and handed it to Maureen.

'Rub its head.'

She hesitated.

'Rub it! Do it now!' he insisted.

'But why, ' she stammered, as she did as she was told.

'Now - throw it away,' he cried, as the flood took him. The last thing he saw was her staring after him, the nail in her hand.

They found his body further down the valley. Maureen brought him home for burial. She was surprised to find herself a rich woman. Nigel had never told her of the lottery win. She was not sure what to do with the old rusty nail he had given her in that last moment. She thought he had said something about throwing it away, and yet - it was his last gift to her. In the end she dropped it into his grave.

Lucky for some

I'm very good at my job. Everyone says so. I take my responsibilities very seriously. And I'm popular. I mean, most Guide Dogs only have one master all their lives, and I'm onto my fifth already! Lucky's the name, and I am lucky too. Four accidents I've been in, and never a scratch on me.

None of them were my fault! I'm very highly trained. I know exactly what to do in any emergency. It's a pity they don't train humans to the same standard. Take that bus driver, for example. He was supposed to stop. Just by where we tried to cross there was a sign clearly saying BUS STOP. How was I to know he was on his way back to the depot?

Owner number two was the headstrong type. Thought she knew better than me. Alright, I know we shouldn't have been on that pier in the first place, but anyone can take a wrong turning. I tried to warn her, but would she listen? Just strode off so confidently I thought, well, she must know what she's doing. And I jumped in to save her, just like a good dog should, but she kept fighting me off. As if she thought I was trying to drown her.

Number three was another stubborn type. In dangerous places like station platforms we are supposed to keep between our master and the edge, but would he have it? No, he liked to have me on his other side, and when it comes down to it, a good dog does what his master tells him. I am a very good dog. I am also courteous, and when I see a lady coming along loaded down with parcels and dragging a litter of children I move out of her way, politely. Only we were rather near the edge and the train just coming in. It was all very unfortunate, not to say messy, but at the enquiry I was completely exonerated.

I'm afraid people were not quite so understanding after number four. I admit, the rules say one should wait for the road to be clear before leading one's owner across - but have you seen the traffic nowadays? You'd be stuck on the kerb forever. You have to take your chance, but it needs perfect trust between owner and dog. That's what went wrong last time. I had a feeling there was trouble coming when I saw that visitor she had. I recognised him from my time with number three. I don't know what he told her, but the next time we went out I could tell he'd really managed to undermine her confidence in me. And the middle of a main road with a truck bearing down on you is no place to start having doubts! If only she'd stuck with me, instead of panicking and trying to run back, we'd have been fine. As it was, she nearly got us both run over.

After that there were some who pointed the finger at me. There was even a suggestion that I should be Put Down, but my trainer still had faith in me. He said I was the best he'd ever trained, and I could not be held responsible for circumstances beyond my control. So they've given me another chance. I'm fine, you see, as long as nothing makes me nervous, and I'm only nervous if my owner is.

That's why they haven't told my new owner anything about me. They've sent me right away, into the country, where there's no busy roads and railways and suchlike hazards. I'm not likely to meet anyone I know, either. So far it's gone really well. He's a nice old gentleman, tall, white hair, very distinguished. And he does just as he's told, unlike some. This evening I thought I'd take him back along the canal, as a treat. It's lovely and peaceful here, and the towpath's nice and dry, except for a bit of mud under the bridge we're just coming to. Have to move him right up to the edge, 'cos the arch is higher there. Dear me, he's taller than I thought.

Duck, you fool!

Oops.

Off shot

Funny, isn't it, the way things turn out. How something quite small can send events careering in one direction or another. They don't reckon anything to me now, I'm just an old man by the fire, drivelling on about the past. But I was a warrior once. I maybe changed the course of history!

It was when I was in England for the 1066 season. Me and my mate Fulk, we were with Duke William's lot. He reckoned he should be king of England. The old king, Edward, had promised him he could, and on top of that he'd got one of the chief men in the kingdom to support him. At least, he thought he had. A few years back, this bloke Harold had been shipwrecked off the Normandy coast, and William had him to stay. Very good friends they were, in fact

William got so fond of him he wouldn't let him go. Not till Harold had sworn to give him the crown, anyway.

Only when he got home, he went back on his word. Soon as old Edward popped his clogs, Harold grabbed the crown for himself. Can't trust anyone nowadays, can you? Naturally, we weren't taking that lying down. We had to go over and sort Harold out.

Duke William called us all together and said, 'Okay lads. The honour of the Normans is at stake. Not to mention some very desirable real estate. You stick with me and I'll see you right. Also, I happen to know the England squad is up north at the moment, playing the Danes. With a bit of luck they'll annihilate each other, or the winner will be too knackered to take us on. Either way, we'll walk it.'

The trip over was pretty horrible, packed into small boats, men and horses all puking their hearts out. It's no joke getting vomit out of chain mail, I can tell you. And that stupid comet in the sky overhead, and everyone saying it presaged a famous victory. Yes, I thought, but does it say whose?

Just as well Harold was otherwise engaged when we arrived. Gave us a chance to recover. We put in the time with a little rape and pillage. Dirty work, but someone's got to do it. Then one morning a messenger rides up shouting 'Harold's here!'.

The English army was drawn up along the top of the ridge. Considering they'd fought a battle not a week before and marched all the way from Yorkshire, they were in pretty good shape. And from the look of them, decidedly peeved.

So battle commenced. The tactics were fairly basic. We charged up the hill, knights on horseback to the fore, us infantry following behind. The idea was for the knights to break through the enemy line, and for us to go in after to mop up. Didn't quite work out like that.

The home team always has the advantage, you see. They held firm and kept throwing us back. So we'd run off pretending to be beaten, hoping to tempt them down from the hill. Nothing doing, they weren't stupid. Back and to it went, with arrows flying around everywhere, it was downright dangerous. We were losing a fair number, the whole thing was starting to look a bit dodgy.

About noon both sides knocked off for a rest. Well, you try fighting all day in armour and hung around with sword and shield and spear - you'd want a breather now and again.

Fulk dug me in the ribs. 'Hey, Ranulf, cover my back, will you? I need to find a bush'

'You should have gone before we started,' I said.

'Sorry. Too much mead at breakfast.'

We sneaked off into the woods bordering the battlefield. Then we had a sit down while we waited for the battle to get going again, and I don't know how it happened, but I must have dozed off. The next thing I remember was Fulk clutching my arm. I froze. I could hear guttural voices nearby. The English line must have moved forward, because there in front of us, screened by trees but barely fifty yards away was a group of thanes and in the midst of them - Harold himself! Big bloke with a droopy moustache. Couldn't miss him.

Fulk had his bow with him, never went anywhere without it. He fancied himself as a marksman, his party trick was splitting an apple on someone's head, and he managed it nine times out of ten. He crept forward, fitting an arrow to the string. I picked up my spear and followed.

To this day I don't know how it happened. Mind you, spears aren't too clever in woodland. The shaft of mine got itself tangled up with my feet, I pitched forward and we ended up in a heap with Fulk underneath. God knows where the arrow went. Next thing, we heard the English go galloping off down the hill, King Harold leading the charge.

The rest is history. Everyone knows how Harold slew William in single combat, before driving the Norman army into the sea. Fulk and I nearly didn't make it back to the boats. The journey back was even more miserable than the one out - there was more room, and the weather had cleared up, but we were all sick as parrots nonetheless.

Fulk never forgave me. 'I had him,' he'd moan. 'I bloody had him. Perfect shot. Couldn't miss. We'd have had it made. Snug little manor in the Home Counties somewhere. If it wasn't for you and your big feet.'

Can't be helped now. And he might have missed anyway. But it just goes to show, doesn't it? Little things.

Makes you think.

Mr Mablethorpe's Hair

Mr Mablethorpe was very sensitive about his hair - and the less he had the more sensitive he became. He grew it very long at one side, and draped the strands over his shining dome, daring anyone to notice it did not quite have the desired effect. He dreaded passing small boys in the street, in case one shouted 'Hey, baldy!' at him.

One blustery day he was walking home from his work at the Spendeazy Furnishing Emporium. He had just turned off the High Street when a fierce gust of wing swept off his hat (he never went out hatless) and sent it spinning away. Worse than that, it lifted his hair from his scalp and set it flapping, banner like. Mr Mablethorpe was mortified. He was far too embarrassed to chase after his hat. All he wanted was to hide his shame.

He happened to be standing outside a small shop which he had never noticed before. Without further ado he dived inside.

'May I assist you, sir?' The tinkle of the shop's bell had summoned the shopkeeper.

'Oh, er, just looking,' mumbled Mr Mablethorpe. He stood, catching his breath and smoothing his ruffled locks, and looked around.

It was a very peculiar shop, full of all sorts of odds and ends: clay pipes, blow-pipes, stuffed alligators, elephant's foot snuffboxes etc. Mr Mablethorpe's attention was caught by a small bottle on a shelf in the corner.

Professor Hirsuto's Magic Hair Encourager it said on the label. *Recommended by the Crowned Heads of Europe.*

'Very good stuff, that,' said the shopkeeper. 'Just the thing for a gentleman who's a bit follically challenged. Makes hair grow anywhere.'

'Hmm. How much?' said Mr Mablethorpe.

'Two guineas - and cheap at the price.'

'Pardon?'

'That'll be two pound fifty.'

Mr Mablethorpe frowned - something was not quite right - but handed over his money anyway.

Before retiring for the night, he read the instructions carefully. *Apply generously, night and morning,* said the label. *Results within days or money refunded.*

'Fair enough, thought Mr Mablethorpe. He opened the bottle and sniffed. 'Phew.' It was powerful

197

stuff, obviously. He poured some into the palms of his hands and massaged it vigorously into his scalp, then went to bed.

He did the same twice a day for the next three days, and on the third day was delighted to observe a definite fuzziness appearing. Once it had started, there was no stopping it. It grew an inch the first day, two inches the second - by the third it was growing over his collar and a visit to the barber was called for. But the more it was cut the more it grew. It was costing him a fortune in hairdressing.

There was worse to come. All the places which the lotion had touched, such as the palms of his hands, began to sprout as well. And it must have got into his bloodstream, because hair started growing in places which had never been in contact with the ghastly fluid - his beard and eyebrows were affected, likewise his chest and legs, and even more intimate areas. We will draw a veil over his ears and nostrils.

'Enough is enough,' he declared at last. 'Something must be Done!'

So he went back to the shop. Only - it wasn't there.

From then on Mr Mablethorpe really went downhill. He lost his job: the management said it put customers off, to come into the shop and encounter a Yeti. His wife said he was no longer the man she had married, and left him. His house was repossessed and he found himself on the streets. The only bright spot was that all the hair helped to keep him warm at night.

Then one day he was in a part of town he had never visited before, when looming through the mist, to his astonishment - he saw it! The shop, the very same.

Salvation at last! With a glad cry he stumbled towards it.

At that exact moment the Great Dipswich Earthquake struck. The ground heaved like an upset stomach. Mr Mablethorpe battled on, but just as he was about to reach his goal, an enormous crack opened in the earth and the entire shop disappeared into it. At the same time he was hit on the head by a flying water closet and knew no more.

Strangely enough, his life then took a turn for the better. He benefited from the Fund for Earthquake Victims, found somewhere to live and eventually a new job.

And best of all - maybe it was the shock - all his hair fell out.

Old bones

It was Sawnoff who first sniffed them out. Because his nose was nearest the ground, probably. We were lurking under the rhododendrons in Corona Park, waiting for the Grub Lady, when suddenly Sawnoff darted to one side and began digging. We wandered over to see what was going on.

He could certainly shift some earth when he'd a mind to. We all got caught up in the excitement. Logdog dropped his stick and joined in; even Fragrant Fanny deigned to lend a paw, while I hopped around the perimeter shouting encouragement. There were some long white things sticking out of the soil at the bottom of the hole. Sawnoff got his teeth round one and dragged it out.

It was a bone.

'Not much meat on that,' said Fanny.

We looked at Big Dick. He's the biggest of us, and the oldest. He doesn't bark often, but when he does, you listen.

'That's no good to us.' he said at last. 'That's a yuman bean. Can't eat yuman beans.'

Sawnoff was a bit put out, but then we got the first whiff of the Grub Lady coming across the park. Her scraps were tastier than any old bones. We raced towards her over the grass. In the rush Logdog got mixed up, and grabbed the bone instead of his stick. I don't think the Grub Lady likes bones much, because when we got close she gave a great shriek, dropped her carrier bags and legged it out of the park as fast as she could go.

By the time we'd finished what was in the bags, the park was full of pleecemen. We don't like pleecemen, so we hid under the brambles on the embankment, and watched what went on. There were cars everywhere, and blue flashing lights. Everyone was kept out of the park, even the walkiedogs and their yuman beans had to stay behind a barrier. Logdog was bothering all the time about his stick. He didn't feel right without something in his mouth.

'Lovely bit of elm, that was,' he whined. 'One of those pleecemen will nick it, for sure.'

What he thought a pleeceman would want with his stick I don't know. But Logdog's obsessed with sticks. I don't know how many he has in his den. Four or five foot long some of them. Takes him hours, some mornings, deciding which one to carry.

As darkness fell the activity quietened down. After a while all the cars went away, leaving only a white tent over our hole. Big Dick stood up and peered out over the park.

'Flea,' he said to me, 'nip over and see what's going on.'

They call me the Flea 'cos I'm small and jump around a lot. I don't mind - they're good lads and look out for me. It's not much fun being undersized and on your own. So I went back across the park and had a look in the tent thing. The flap was open, and inside the pleeceman was sitting in a chair, keeping guard with his eyes shut and his mouth open. Our hole was bigger now, and they'd gone off with all the bones. Can't think why. Like Fanny said, there was no meat on them.

Logdog's stick was there, lying where he had dropped it. I yipped a couple of times to tell the others to come over, and soon they padded up out of the darkness.

'Are you going in to get it?' asked Fragrant Fanny.

Logdog hesitated. I could see it was agony for him, having his stick so near and yet so far, but what if the pleeceman woke up? Pleecemen are as bad as Dogsnatchers, they all want to shove you in a cage and cut your nuts off. We stay well clear of them.

Sawnoff wrinkled his nose. 'Someone coming,' he said.

We could hear him. No matter how quiet yuman beans try to be, they sound like a herd of rhinoceroses to us. Sawnoff's nose was still twitching. He's by far the best smeller in the gang. I think there must be some bloodhound in him, though he looks like a collie with its legs sawn off.

'Funny,' he muttered, 'I know that scent, it was all round the hole - he's the one who buried the bones! He must be coming back for them.'

We lay doggo as the bean blundered towards us, not looking where he was going. They never do. Then if he didn't put one of his great feet right on Fanny's tail. She leapt up with a heart-rending squeal, Big Dick gave one of his deep reverberating barks, and I nipped in and bit the bean on the ankle. I couldn't help myself, the excitement got to me. Inside the tent the pleeceman woke up with a start, his chair wobbled and went over backwards, and he fell into the hole.

Logdog seized his chance to rush into the tent and grab his stick. It was one of his biggest, at least four times longer than he was. Unfortunately on his way out he got it snarled up in the ropes and the tent fell down onto the pleeceman, who was just climbing out of the hole. The bean was in a terrible panic, yelling and kicking out at us, till he tripped over the stick as Logdog dragged it clear of the tent. He fell down. Then the tent rose up and landed on top of him.

'Time to go,' said Big Dick.

I would have stayed (it was a chance to increase my vocabulary) but you don't argue with Big Dick, so we scarpered. We kept away from the park till everything got back to normal, and we've told Sawnoff, if he smells anything like that again, to leave it alone. It's too much hassle, for a lot of old bones.

Bye Bye Blackbird

It was an outrage. A diabolical liberty, that's what it was. I mean, what had we ever done to them? We woke them up with the dawn chorus, every morning, never missed. We gave them a song in the evening as well. Many's the time I saw the king take a break from reckoning up his tax yield, just to listen. The queen used to leave her crusts on the parlour window sill, after she'd finished stuffing herself with bread and honey. We thought they liked us.

Our best friend, as we thought, was the laundry maid. Every morning she'd come into the palace yard to hang out the washing, and she'd have her pocket full of rye to scatter for us. We got to look for her. When she was due there'd be a crowd of us on the fence, not just blackbirds, but starlings, sparrows, chaffinches, even a robin or two, all sitting there with our beaks open.

We knew there was a big feast planned for the king's birthday. We were looking forward to it. Whenever the court has a good blow-out, there'll always be plenty of pickings left over for us. We little thought …

The big day dawned. We gave his Majesty a specially rousing chorus at 4.30am to mark the occasion. Then we went off to wait for the maid to bring us our breakfast. She must be feeling generous this morning, we thought, because she'd brought two pocketfuls of rye this time. She went in, and no sooner had we got properly stuck in -

Someone went and dropped a bloody great net on us!

You never heard such a screeching and a twittering and a chattering! A couple of nasty little boys started to disentangle us from the net - I'd have liked to say we got a few pecks in, but I think most of us were too scared to do anything. They let the sparrows and other riff-raff go, but all us blackbirds they put in a cage. Twenty-four of us they had in the end. They took us to the back door of the palace, and when one of the scullery maids answered, they said, 'We got the blackbirds - where's our sixpence?'

Sixpence! That's all we were worth to them. It was an insult. Didn't they realise I'd won Bird Songster of the Year three times? That should have been good for a shilling, in itself. But worse was to come. As the girl carried us in we heard her shout, 'Here they are, chef! The blackbirds for the pie.'

Of course, we'd heard that in some countries they ate blackbirds, but we'd always thought it was a nasty foreign habit. Not British. What was the world coming to? Perhaps it had something to do with being in Europe now. We gave ourselves up for lost.

I don't know how long we waited before someone came and put us into a large pie dish. Next thing, the top was sealed with a great wodge of puff pastry, and we were shoved in the oven. Now, I'm not saying we were actually baked. We were only in long enough to brown the top a bit. But it got very hot and airless, not to mention dark and crowded, and I'm sure I don't need to remind you of the effect extreme terror has on the bowels. Suffice it to say, it was not pleasant in there. Not pleasant at all.

After a while we felt the pie dish being moved, carried along then put down. Trumpets blared faintly though the pie crust. Suddenly we could see daylight as a knife broke through the pastry, and there was the king staring down at us, looking ever so surprised.

They said as the pie was opened we started singing. You must be bloody joking. We could barely croak. We got out of there fast enough, all the same. We were all terribly bewildered and disorientated, we had a job finding our way out of the hall. One or two flew into the windows and stunned themselves, and one poor young bird, scarcely more than a fledgling, was so frightened she flopped on the floor and couldn't move. I think the cat got her. Most of us made it out of the door in the end. Quite a few of the courtiers got strafed on the way, and I wouldn't have fancied the sherry trifle, myself. I personally bombed the queen's new dress, and from the look on her face, I don't think the chef will be baking blackbird pie again, soon.

My nerves have recovered pretty well, considering, though I'll never be the bird I was. I don't go near the palace any more. Dawn chorus? They can stuff it! I did manage to get my own back on that laundry maid. As soon as I felt up to it I flew back and waited for her to come out with the washing. While she had her hands full, I swooped down and gave her a good peck on the nose. Some say that I pecked it right off. That's rubbish. I don't have a big enough pecker. Still, she didn't half squeal!

But I haven't been able to touch a grain of rye, since.

Lightning Source UK Ltd.
Milton Keynes UK
UKOW040443080313

207327UK00001B/5/P